WHISPERING PINES RANCH novel

Lorcan's Desire

"Peterson rocked the angst, and I loved every word of it."

"...this b
left hangi

: have been

"Despite
And thou
finds his

)ut Lorcan.
know if he

"Peterson
and an ex

characters

A WHISPERING PINES RANCH NOVEL

TY'S
OBSESSION

SJD PETERSON

Published by
Dreamspinner Press
382 NE 191st Street #88329
Miami, FL 33179-3899, USA
http://www.dreamspinnerpress.com/

Ty's Obsession

Cover art by Don Porter
Cover design by Anne Cain

ISBN: 978-1-61372-353-1

Printed in the United States of America
First Edition
February 2012

eBook edition available
eBook ISBN: 978-1-61372-354-8

You have been with me since the first book in this series. Your proofreading, opinions, and encouragement have meant the world to me. I love you, Jason Bradley, and I dedicate this book to you!

AUTHOR'S NOTES

Ty's Obsession is the third book in the Whispering Pines Ranch series. To fully understand what is happening in each story, the novels must be read in order. The first book is *Lorcan's Desire*. The second book is *Quinn's Need*. The series is available from Dreamspinner Press.

Thank you for reading *Ty's Obsession*. I hope you enjoy it!

Jo

PROLOGUE

ANGER, desire, jealousy, longing—all battled against each other for supremacy, leaving Ty shaking and a little unsteady on his feet. He leaned against the jamb of the barn door to steady himself as the war inside his heart and head raged. How the hell had he gotten here? No connections, no emotions, and no complications, that had been his motto. Yet here he stood staring out into the barnyard as Conner went up to Quinn, a large smile on Conner's old and weathered face, and Ty's chest tightened painfully at the sight of Quinn. For a moment, desire and longing moved to the forefront as he watched Conner say something to Quinn and a brilliant smile bloomed across Quinn's face. To Ty, the smile was like a match to a torch, heating him. God, Quinn was so gorgeous, so very sexy standing there in the tight Levi's that accentuated his perfect ass. A black T-shirt stretched tightly across his impressive bulk, showing each valley and ridge of his muscular back and chest. But that smile, that magnificent, happy smile on Quinn's handsome face touched Ty deep inside, and for a moment, he lost himself in the pleasure that smile elicited. For a split second, all the anger and pain melted away, and Ty couldn't help but smile in return. Then, like the sun coming out from behind a cloud, Quinn's smile turned radiant, and he lifted a hand and waved. Ty turned his head in the direction Quinn was staring, and pain, raw and consuming, ripped through him, causing his knees to buckle, and he leaned more heavily against the door to keep from falling.

   Lorcan.

Ty turned his gaze back to Quinn, watching as the man continued to talk with Conner, his smile still broad and his eyes never leaving Lorcan. Why did Lorcan have to come back to town? If he'd just stayed gone, Quinn would still be Ty's. This pain shredding his chest was why he never let anyone get close to him. He had learned as a small boy that caring about people caused pain much more consequential than any physical injury ever could. A bullwhip in the hands of a skilled Dom gave him the most pleasurable pain. A confident master could make him scream and send him flying to such heights he could soar out of his body, out of his head. That kind of pain he understood. Skin splitting, muscles straining, and flesh bruising, that kind of suffering he not only understood but also craved. This… this agony that was compressing his heart so tightly he couldn't breathe, Ty didn't understand at all. He couldn't use a salve or ice pack or even rest for a few days to give his body time to heal. No amount of pain reliever or alcohol could completely drown out what he felt as he watched Quinn look at Lorcan with that smile on his face.

A lump formed in Ty's throat as he watched Conner hug Quinn, then head back toward the house. He knew what it felt like to hug that hard body, to be in Quinn's embrace, and he longed to feel it again. When Quinn started to walk toward Lorcan, Ty shook his head, silently pleading that Quinn not go to him.

As if Quinn had heard his plea, he stopped and turned his head toward Ty, and their eyes met. For a moment, Ty let himself believe that Quinn was choosing him over Lorcan. Quinn was his, and he'd come to Ty, tell him he was sorry, that he'd made a terrible mistake running to Lorcan and wanted Ty back. The smile on Quinn's face fell, and the fantasy was snatched away.

Pity.

Pity, understanding, and apology were what he saw staring back at him in Quinn's blue eyes, but not a shred of desire or want. Ty's stomach rolled and bile burned the back of his throat, and just like that, the anger reared its ugly head and the battle turned in its favor. He crossed his arms over his chest and glared at Quinn. *Don't you dare fucking pity me.* He'd seen that look on the faces of his teachers when he was a kid, sometimes in the tired eyes of the social worker who came to remove him from one shithole, knowing they were sending him to another. He would not tolerate that look from anyone, especially Quinn.

Quinn made a move as if to come to him. *No the fuck you don't.* Ty spun away from the door and stomped off toward the other side of the barn. His boots eating up the dirt and dust, he let his anger propel his body forward until he was out the door on the opposite side of the barn, and he didn't stop until he reached a small grove of trees. His breath coming in short, harsh pants, he paced and raged until he collapsed against the base of a wide oak. He drew his knees up and hung his head. "Fucking Quinn!" he groaned.

Ty inhaled deeply, struggling to find some calm. He was surrounded by the scents of fresh-cut hay, wide-open fields, and grazing animals, and that should have been enough to calm him. When he had been a boy, they had had a calming effect on him, and he tried to find that calm now. He hadn't had many opportunities to enjoy life in the country back then, but he'd gotten lucky a couple of times to get foster families who owned small ranches, and they had been some of the best times of his life. Those families hadn't been any better than the ones he lived with in the city; they took him in not because they gave a rat's ass about an abandoned kid but for free labor. Still, he'd learned to ride, muck stalls, and care for the livestock, and he'd loved the tranquility of the country and working with his hands. He'd been given three square meals a day and a roof over his head, and as long as he worked hard, the owners didn't bother him too much. It sure beat the hell out of the inner city projects. He shuddered. Those had been a fucking nightmare. *That train of thought isn't helping,* he chastised himself and leaned his head back against the tree. *Just breathe.*

Rolling his shoulders, trying to release some of the tension, Ty took in another deep breath of the sweet scent. Unfortunately, it was going to take a hell of a lot more than the sights and sounds of a cattle ranch to calm him. Nothing was soothing him these days. To make matters worse, he didn't even have the release he sought from The Push. He'd given up working there all but one day a week to help Quinn out. It didn't matter that Marcus had been about to cut his hours back; he could have found another gig with one of the other leather bars, maybe even gotten into one of the private clubs, but no. No, his stupid ass had to go and offer to help out the arrogant son of a bitch, Quinn, and what the fuck had he gotten in return?

Ty removed his hat and ran a hand through his sweat-dampened hair. *I'll tell you what it got me: not a fucking thing!*

Well… that wasn't entirely true, now was it? One too many times leaving early for Quinn, only going in the back rooms with Quinn, and spending his one night a week behind the bar waiting for Quinn instead of working the crowd had gotten him a real pretty pink slip.

Life may not have been all that great before Quinn walked in the door of The Push that first time, but it hadn't sucked as much as it did now. He had been content going about his business, flirting with the customers, and had had a sweet list of Doms who requested him and knew exactly what he liked. His life had been completely uncomplicated until that sexy son of a bitch walked into The Push and said, *"Join me on the dance floor if you got a break coming anytime soon."* That first night hadn't been much more than a blowjob in the alleyway, but Ty had known instantly that he'd never met anyone quite like the arrogant cowboy, and he'd been right. Quinn had swept into his life like a whirlwind, leaving him with only the memory of his taste and touch, but Christ, it had been enough to produce some hot fantasies. He'd given up hope of ever seeing him again, but he had been one happy bastard that he'd been wrong. Just thinking about how Quinn had fucked him that first time had his heart beating hard in his chest and his dick throbbing as the images solidified in his mind. No one had ever made him fly like Quinn or given him what he'd needed so badly.

Just as quickly as the blood had run south, it raced to his head, causing it to throb with a new kind of agony when he thought of how his body hadn't been the only thing Quinn had dominated. No, the fucker had to force Ty to feel something more than just the pleasurable pain, something he swore he'd never allow anyone to do. His hands tightened into fists, crushing his hat as he struggled against the anger ripping through him, but it held him in its grip. *My body wasn't enough, was it, Quinn?* Ty's muscles tightened, and his breath became harsh. "You just had to fucking dominate my heart too, didn't you," Ty cried out with labored breaths. "Fucking hell!" Oh, God, he was coming unhinged, thoughts of Quinn rocketing from one extreme to the other, leaving him struggling to keep up.

You'd have thought Brian would have taught your stupid ass not to let your heart make any of the goddamn decisions. Ty slapped his hat against his knee and angrily plopped it back on his head. Yeah, well, he wasn't all that damn smart, was he? Sitting here having a conversation with himself was proof positive of that. Besides, he was sick and tired of comparing Quinn and Brian. They were nothing alike. Brian had been an uncaring, sadistic prick who took advantage of a kid with nowhere to go, and Quinn... well, Quinn wasn't anything like him. Even when Quinn had been full of rage, walking into The Push with a huge chip on his shoulder and his don't-fuck-with-me attitude, there had been an underlying goodness to the man. The way Quinn had gently helped him to bed, tended to his back with soft, soothing touches of his fingers as he worked salve into Ty's wounds. Ty had always known Quinn was a good man, completely different from anyone he'd ever met, and no way in hell was he going to step back and let Lorcan have him. Quinn was his.

Ah, Lorcan. That one word summed up all his problems and gave Ty a moment of true clarity. If it weren't for Lorcan coming back, Ty would still have Quinn. The guy was sexy, he'd give him that. Ty had never seen hair quite like that before, at least not on a dude, but from what he could tell, Lorcan's hair was the only thing that made him special. The immature little shit sure didn't deserve someone like Quinn. He just needed to figure out how to get rid of his little *problem.*

What to do, what to do, he asked himself as he tapped a finger against his knee. Focusing on Lorcan was helping him find a balance for his out-of-control emotions. Lorcan was the root of his problem, and getting him out of the picture was the one thing both his mind and body agreed upon.

From what Quinn had told him, Lorcan was the kind who ran when things got rough. Ty liked rough, was in fucking heaven when things got very rough. He sure as hell wouldn't run. Oh no, he'd be on his knees begging, submitting to Quinn's brutal side. Quinn could deny his harsher tendencies all he wanted, but Ty had felt the power, the excitement in those strokes. He'd seen the look in Quinn's eyes, heard the roar of his release and felt his pleasure when he was dominating a lover.

Quinn needed to dominate.

He needed Ty.

Pulling himself to his feet, Ty dusted off the seat of his jeans and headed back toward the ranch. A smile curled his lips as a calm feeling began to spread through him. He'd just have to make things *rough* for Lorcan.

CHAPTER
ONE

RIBBONS of the softest silk tickled against Quinn's side and along his arm. The perfect weight pressed down on his side as gentle lips teased down his neck to his breastbone, bringing him out of his light sleep. Quinn wrapped his arms around Lorcan, moaning softly as his hands slid through the silky strands of his lover's hair and pulled him harder against his chest.

Blinking, he placed a kiss to the top of Lorcan's head. "Mmm, it's still dark, go back to sleep," he murmured.

"Can't," Lorcan whispered against his chest, the warmth of his breath tickling Quinn's skin. "I got to get home. I got chores to do."

Quinn groaned and pulled Lorcan up and took a kiss, encouraging Lorcan to lie fully on top of him. "I hate that word," he complained. He let his hands roam down Lorcan's back to the firm globes of his ass and pulled him hard against his lengthening shaft.

Lorcan hissed at the contact but pushed harder against Quinn, rolling his hips. "What word—chores? You're in the wrong business, then, cowboy," Lorcan teased.

"No, when you refer to Jess's ranch as home."

Lorcan leaned back, the full moon shining in through the window lighting up the fierce look in the man's eyes. "You're not jealous of Jess, are you? We've—"

Quinn cupped the back of Lorcan's head and pulled him down for a kiss, silencing him. "No, I'm not jealous," he whispered against Lorcan's lips when the kiss ended. He encouraged him to lie back down until Lorcan's head was resting on his shoulder. "I just wish you'd move in here. Consider this ranch your home, our home."

"Quinn," Lorcan responded softly, "we've talked about this. It's only been a few weeks, and besides, I told you, I have to keep Jess's ranch going until he gets home."

"We'll hire someone to run the ranch. Hell, I'm sure we could get Collin to stay there at night."

It was Lorcan's turn to silence him with a kiss, his tongue teasing until Quinn opened up and welcomed him in. His lover kissed him deeply, pulling a moan from deep in his chest and effectively cutting off any further conversation. With the press of Lorcan's naked body and his flavor exploding on his tongue, nothing else mattered. Lorcan kissed him so thoroughly that Quinn was dazed when it ended, and it took his brain a moment to catch up to what was happening. The next thing he knew, Lorcan was padding across the floor, his tight butt demanding Quinn follow. Who was he to disobey such a command?

"That wasn't very nice," Quinn complained as he stepped into the shower stall behind Lorcan. "No fair using this gorgeous body and that talented tongue to frazzle my brain." He grabbed the body in question and tugged.

Lorcan chuckled and allowed Quinn to pull him against him. "It's the only way I can get my way with you."

"Mmm," Quinn moaned, nuzzling the side of Lorcan's neck. "You can have your way with me all you want, preferably your wicked way."

God, the man felt amazing in Quinn's arms. He still had a hard time believing that he had him back. The nightmares were nearly nonexistent these days, but there had been a few nights he'd woken in a panic. He didn't remember the dream but had a damn good idea what it had been about. Funny thing—it only happened on the few nights he and Lorcan didn't share a bed. He'd had to put his foot down on that subject. If Lorcan couldn't sleep in his bed for whatever reason, Quinn went to Lorcan's; it was as simple as that.

Quinn grabbed the soap and began to run the bar down Lorcan's chest, causing a pleasurable sound to rumble from his lover. He washed Lorcan's body quickly, lingering only a little longer than necessary on

Lorcan's more sensitive parts. He loved how Lorcan leaned into his touch, the sweet sounds that escaped him, and, even more, loved that he could do this. He added shampoo to Lorcan's thick waves, working it in, enjoying the way the chestnut strands felt against his skin.

"Love you," he murmured against the side of Lorcan's neck. He licked at the water droplets and felt the man shudder.

"Love you too," Lorcan replied, followed by a satisfied groan as Quinn moved his hands up and worked the shampoo deep into Lorcan's scalp.

Stepping back, he pushed Lorcan toward the flow of warm water, running his fingers through the silky strands until the water ran clear. He then added a generous amount of conditioner and turned Lorcan in his arms. With the length and thickness of Lorcan's hair, the conditioner worked better when it had time to set a bit, giving Quinn the perfect opportunity to play and have a little fun with his lover.

Quinn grabbed Lorcan's ass and pulled him hard against him. "So what's the plan for the day? Can I suggest my personal favorite pastime, stay in bed all day or... stay in bed all day?"

"Those are hard to choose between." Lorcan chuckled. "As much as I'd love to stay in bed with you all day—" He kissed Quinn's lips, pulling away slightly. "—I'll have to go with plan C. You know how Bunny gets when he doesn't get his breakfast in a timely manner."

Quinn lifted his brow and tried for a pout. "I can't believe you're picking that hateful bull over me." From the way Lorcan laughed, he was pretty sure his pout didn't have the same effect as Lorcan's did. Instead of getting what he wanted, he was handed a washcloth.

Lorcan rinsed his hair quickly. "I'd return the favor and wash you, but I know you too well. I'd be spending the afternoon repairing the damage a hungry bull caused in his starvation rampage." Lorcan placed one last chaste kiss to Quinn's lips and stepped out of the shower.

"Fine," he said grudgingly as he began to wash his own body. By himself, with no help. *Stupid bull!* "I'm coming with you."

"I would hope so," Lorcan called out as he left the bathroom.

A thought occurred to him, and Quinn yelled out, "Don't even think about touching that brush."

He washed quickly, hearing Lorcan chuckle from the other room. *Go ahead and laugh*, he thought to himself. He was getting damn good at finding all of Lorcan's weak spots, and a huge one was having his hair brushed. There was just something about having Lorcan between his spread legs and running his hands through those thick locks, turning his lover into a moaning, pliable pile of I'm-so-easy goo. Quinn turned off the taps and stepped out of the shower with a big smile on his face. *Oh yeah, I'm so getting laid before Bunny gets his breakfast.*

THE scowl that used to confuse and anger Lorcan now tickled him when Quinn tried using it on him. He'd known exactly what Quinn was up to when he'd yelled at him not to touch the brush. Quinn was still trying to learn his buttons. Funny that the man hadn't figured that Lorcan's weakness was Quinn. No matter how the man touched him or looked at him, Lorcan just melted, but today he'd held firm. He'd gotten dressed and started twisting his hair into a quick braid before Quinn could even make it out of the bathroom, hence the scowl on his face.

"Haven't you ever heard the saying 'If it's good, it's worth waiting for'?"

"Sure I have," Quinn said gruffly. He stomped toward the closet and grabbed a pair of jeans, pulling them on with a wince before continuing. "I'm more of the 'practice makes perfect' school of thought."

"Just imagine how much more fun we'll have practicing later after a day of anticipation." Lorcan couldn't help but smile as Quinn huffed out a breath and finished dressing.

Quinn was still grumbling as he followed him into the kitchen, but Lorcan didn't tease his cranky lover further, just led him to the back door and grabbed his boots. The quicker they got the chores done, the quicker they could get back. There wasn't too much that could pull him away from Quinn, and he rarely ever told the man no—didn't *want* to tell him no. His dominant lover was demanding, intense, and Lorcan loved every minute of it. Being the sole focus of a man like Quinn was beyond good, it was fucking mind-blowing. However, this morning Conner was more important than even Quinn's needs.

Conner wasn't sleeping well, and although he tried to deny it, Lorcan could see it in his bloodshot eyes and the dark circles under them. The man tried to act as if there was nothing wrong, but the way he carried himself, the light missing from his eyes, gave him away. Usually Conner was so full of life—hell, he was bigger than life, laughing, joking, and caring for those around him. Now he just seemed so exhausted, and John was the reason.

John's back wasn't getting any better. Lorcan heard the pain-filled moans as John made his way to the bathroom at night, yet the stubborn ol' coot refused to take it easy. Worse still, John refused to go back to the doctor. Conner wasn't the only one that was worried sick. John looked worn to the bone. Lorcan wasn't an expert by any stretch, but even he knew the sickly pallor of John's skin wasn't right. There was something seriously wrong with John, and Lorcan was beside himself with anxiety. He was going to have himself a chat with the cranky ol' thing, and hopefully he could make John see reason. He wasn't above doing a little begging, pouting a little, if need be, and if all else failed, he would make John feel guilty for making Conner worry enough that he was missing meals and losing sleep. John just had to get better. There wasn't any alternative. It would kill Conner if anything happened to him.

Shaking off the sickening feeling, Lorcan stomped into his boots, grabbed his hat from the hook, and headed out the back door.

"C'mon, Quinn, if we get back here before Conner gets up so I can help him make breakfast, we'll take a long lunch and get some practicing in."

Quinn whooped, a smile that Lorcan felt all the way to his toes blooming across his handsome face. Chuckling at his eager lover, he headed for his truck.

What the fuck?

Quinn nearly knocked him down when Lorcan came to an abrupt halt a few yards from his truck. His shock was so profound it scattered his brain for a moment, and he couldn't make sense of what he was seeing. Then it hit him, and his gut twisted painfully. Written across the windshield in bold white letters was "DISLOYAL BASTARD."

Quinn cursed under his breath, but Lorcan didn't pay him any attention. He was moving toward his truck and reaching for the paper tucked under the windshield wiper. Even in the dim light of early dawn, he recognized the pamphlet. "Tulsa Rehabilitation Center" was printed neatly across the top.

"Get back in the house," Quinn demanded.

Again, Lorcan ignored him. He stared down at the pamphlet from the rehab center where Jess was currently recovering from his accident, and he felt sick to his stomach. The implications were painfully clear. Someone obviously wasn't too happy about the choices he had made. Jess still wasn't talking to him, though Lorcan got regular updates from both Collin and Jack. Jess was standing firm in his declaration that he would walk again, and from what Jack had told him, Jess was sticking to it with a single-minded determination. Lorcan respected Jess's insistence that they not have any contact. He didn't like it, but he respected it.

Lorcan sent updates on Jess's ranch with Collin and never failed to end his conversations with Collin by repeating, "Tell Jess I'm here for him if he needs me and I miss him." He hated the fact that Jess wouldn't talk to him and still wasn't ready to see him. But what could he do? Maybe he should have waited until Jess was on his feet before he had run back to Quinn.

Lorcan crushed the pamphlet in his fist and closed his eyes, but he still saw the words behind closed lids. *Disloyal bastard.* He flinched when a strong arm wrapped around him and pulled him into a tight embrace.

"Don't you dare even think about it," Quinn said adamantly. "It's not true."

Too late. His head and heart at times still debated this very issue. He'd known since the first moment he'd laid eyes on Quinn that there was something special about the man. Was it love at first sight with Quinn? He wasn't sure, but it was pretty damn close. Logically he knew it wasn't as if he'd run out and looked for someone to replace Jess the moment things had gotten tough. He was with the man he'd always loved, the same man Jess knew Lorcan had always been in love with. That didn't stop his heart from hurting from the loss of Jess. It still didn't completely erase the guilt he sometimes felt that it should have been him who'd gone to the hardware store that day. At the end of the day, he had to believe that he was exactly where he was meant to be.

Taking a deep breath, Lorcan released the tight grip he had on the pamphlet and let it fall to the ground. "I'm okay," he reassured Quinn, wrapping his arms around his lover and returning the hug. "Let's get this shit washed off. I got critters to feed."

Quinn squeezed him harder briefly before letting him go. "Damn right we do. You promised me a long lunch if I got you back here before Conner got up, and I aim to collect." Quinn placed a tender kiss on his forehead. "Go grab something to get this off, and I'll make sure there isn't any other vandalism."

Lorcan nodded, knowing it was pointless to argue. No way would Quinn leave him out here alone, and he wasn't in the mood to argue his point that he was more than capable of taking care of himself. He had to learn to pick his battles and sometimes just let Quinn be his protective caveman self. Besides, he had shit to do, and right now wasn't the time to be trying to figure out who in the hell was pissed off at him enough to pull this stunt. He had a sneaking suspicion and was pretty sure Quinn was thinking along the same lines, but Lorcan wasn't about to blame Ty unless he had proof.

CHAPTER
TWO

THE hair on the back of Lorcan's neck stood on end as he walked across the barnyard. He could feel eyes upon him, but every time he turned around, no one was there. He quickened his steps, making his way to the barn. The unease that had settled in his gut yesterday morning hadn't let up. If anything, the feeling had intensified. Maybe it was one of the hands who had been close with Jess who had left the message on his truck and he was suspecting Ty unfairly. Jess sure had his share of supporters; how could the big lovable guy not? Lorcan just wished that if they felt he was doing wrong by Jess they would come and talk to him instead of talking about it behind his back. Looking back, Lorcan could easily admit that he had made a lot of foolish mistakes since first meeting both Jess and Quinn, but he was doing his best to learn from them.

Stepping into the quiet barn, Lorcan felt his edginess increase as he slowly made his way farther into the building, scanning the area for Quinn. When he didn't find his lover, he glanced down at his watch. *12:05.* Quinn was only a few minutes late—not all that unusual, since cattle rarely followed a schedule. Goose bumps suddenly bloomed across his skin, and it wasn't Quinn's tardiness that caused the sensation but the feeling that someone was still watching him. Lorcan rubbed at his arms, hating the way his skin was tingling. *This is getting ridiculous.* Either someone really was watching him or he'd developed one hell of a case of paranoia. The sound of a horse whinnying behind him had Lorcan whipping around, nearly jumping out of his skin. "Jesus, get a grip," he chided himself, his heart beating out of his chest as adrenaline surged through his system, and he chuckled nervously at his scaredy-cat antics. Then a newspaper tacked to the stall caught his attention, and he moved closer to inspect it. All traces of laughter died as the familiar headline came into view.

"Local Man Severely Injured in Head-On Crash."

The article—in and of itself—was hard enough to see. The sight of Jess's mangled truck hit him directly in the center of his chest, stealing his breath, but the words written across the page in glaring black letters clawed at his heart. "At least you got to walk away." Without warning, Lorcan was transported back to Jess's hospital room the first time Jess woke up after the accident.

Jess blinked at him with a blank stare on his face. Lorcan wasn't sure he was really awake or seeing him until the corner of his mouth curled ever so slightly. Lorcan brushed a fingertip over Jess's lips, tracing the slight smile, his own smile blooming across his face.

"Bad dream," Jess tried to say, but it was so low Lorcan could barely make it out. It was more a movement of his lips than any real sound.

Lorcan leaned up, brushed away the hair from Jess's forehead, and kissed it. "Yeah, a really bad dream, but it's over now, and you're awake." He brushed his lips across Jess's. "Are you in pain? Do you need anything?"

"You," Jess replied.

Tears burned Lorcan's eyes. "Ah, God, big guy, you got me. I'm right here and not going anywhere." Jess gave him a real smile that sent a rush of warmth straight to Lorcan's heart.

When the image dissipated, Lorcan was left clutching the stall door for support with tears rolling down his face. He had lied. He had promised he wasn't going anywhere when Jess confessed that he needed him, but he had. He'd run right back to Quinn the moment he got the chance. Had he really tried hard to see Jess after he'd received the letter? He'd thought he'd come to peace with the decisions he'd made, and when he was in Quinn's arms he knew in his soul it was where he belonged, but did he deserve to be there? Did he deserve to be happy when his best friend, the man he'd promised to be there for, was alone and still struggling to walk? The same arguments that his head and heart slung at each other came rushing back, leaving Lorcan dizzy with guilt.

"Hey, babe, you're early," Quinn called out from behind Lorcan.

Lorcan grabbed the newspaper clipping, ripping it from the stall, and crumbled it into a tight ball. Quinn would freak out if he saw it. His protective lover had been ready to interrogate every last man on the ranch and beat the shit out of whoever had left the last message on his truck. It had taken all of Lorcan's persuasive skills, including his pout, to stop Quinn. He couldn't imagine what kind of rant this latest one would send him into.

"Actually, I was five minutes late," Lorcan responded without turning around. He ran a hand across his face, wiping away the last traces of his tears, and took a deep breath.

Quinn came up behind him, wrapping his arms around Lorcan's waist and nuzzling the side of his neck. "It's only a little after eleven. I was planning on surprising you with a really long practice... I mean lunch."

"Eleven?" he questioned. He looked once again at his watch. 12:15. *That's strange,* he thought. *Battery must be dying.* "Guess I'm early."

He didn't think his voice had given him away, but obviously Quinn heard something, because he whirled Lorcan around and asked, "What the hell happened?"

"What do you mean?" He tried to make it sound like Quinn was crazy, that he was still overreacting to what had happened the previous day, but the look in Quinn's eyes told him he couldn't fool the man. Still, there was no way he was going to tell Quinn about the newspaper clipping.

Quinn cupped Lorcan's face in his hands. "Baby, you're shaking and you look as if you've been crying, what do you think I mean?"

"It's nothing, just was thinking about what happened yesterday," he lied.

"You want to talk about it?" Quinn asked, concerned. His thumbs gently stroked Lorcan's cheeks, easing some of his tension.

Lorcan shook his head. "Nah, I'm okay, really. I think I'm just tired." He hadn't slept very well the night before, so that wasn't a complete lie. He was tired, and not just from the lack of sleep. His head hurt, his heart hurt, and he wished he knew how to stop the self-doubt that was creeping its way into his system. "How about we head to the house, skip lunch, and go snuggle?"

Quinn studied him for a moment and then placed a soft kiss on Lorcan's lips. "Okay," he replied, releasing Lorcan's face and wrapping an arm around his waist, "but we're not skipping lunch."

With the way his gut was flopping around like a fish out of water, there was no way he could eat right now. He let Quinn lead him out of the barn, the evidence hidden in his fist. "All right, but let's postpone lunch for an hour. I'm thinking I need the nap more than the food right now."

"You sure you're okay?" Quinn inquired, pulling Lorcan tighter against him as they made their way to the main house.

Not really. "Yeah, I'm good," he reassured Quinn, hugging him back. He could still feel eyes on him, making his skin crawl. A few of the hands who had come in with Quinn turned their heads in his direction, greeting Lorcan with a nod or a small wave. He and Quinn didn't go out of their way to flaunt their relationship in front of others, but it was completely different from the first time he'd been on the ranch. Quinn had settled comfortably into his own skin, and when Quinn hugged him or held his hand around others, it was proof of just how comfortable the man was. No, the eyes he still felt on him were not accepting or friendly eyes. He wasn't sure how he knew; he just did. Either that or his paranoia was still riding him hard, but he had the sneaking suspicion it was the former.

True to his word, Quinn made sure Lorcan had a hearty lunch after their nap. It was more like an hour lying wrapped in Quinn's arms. He didn't really rest, and he sure as hell didn't sleep. The image of Jess's mangled truck kept flashing through his mind, and it took all his willpower not to tense or show any outward signs of the fierce combat his head and heart were still engaged in. It was easier to know he'd made the right decision while he was with Quinn. He loved everything about the man. He loved how Quinn made him feel complete when he was with him, but when he was alone, he felt as if he were between the hammer and the anvil. Indecision and uncertainty seemed to keep him off balance.

Later, after Quinn had gone back out to the yard, Lorcan was once again left alone with his conflicting thoughts. He placed his elbows on the kitchen table and hung his head, his hands sliding through his hair. Fuck! Why did growing up and becoming an adult have to be so goddamn hard?

Everything had been so much simpler before he left home last year. A fight with one of his brothers never lasted long. They'd scream and yell, sometimes even get physical, but they never held a grudge, most times settled their differences and forgave each other before bedtime. The more difficult problems he could always count on Mama to solve. Then again, he had never had issues that had been about the heart. He was learning real fast that those were never simple, and most times someone got hurt and no amount of soothing words from Mama could fix them.

His relationship with Jess was a prime example of a problem that Mama couldn't fix. He'd thought he had put the guilt and uncertainty behind him, but maybe that wasn't the case. The last two days had him questioning every decision he'd made since receiving that letter from Jess. What if Collin was sugarcoating how Jess was so as not to upset Lorcan? He could so see Jess making Collin agree to that. He needed to see Jess for himself. Needed the man to look him in the eye and tell him to his face that everything was okay. Jess couldn't lie; Lorcan would be able to see the truth in those big blue eyes. Lorcan's breath caught as a piercing pain shot through his chest. *Christ! I should have demanded to see him.* What if the good feelings that Quinn brought out overshadowed his judgment and he was being a selfish bastard? Was it possible he couldn't see beyond his own happiness?

You're damn right it's possible. You have everything you've ever wanted. You have Quinn by your side, and he's out of the closet. Teasing about marriage, planning the rest of your life with your true love—and what the fuck does Jess have? You walked away from all that misery, and Jess still hasn't.

The hands in his hair tightened as the questions came faster and faster and faster. He wanted to pull his fucking hair out or beat his fool head on the table until he silenced them. "God, I wish I knew the answers," he groaned.

"You have to ask the questions first, hon."

Lorcan looked up as Conner moved toward him, concern in his tired eyes. "Sorry, didn't realize you were in the room."

Conner gave him a slight smile and took the seat next to him. He gently pulled Lorcan's hand from his hair and entwined their fingers. "So what's the first question?"

Lorcan didn't want to dump all the shit in his head on Conner. The man had enough to worry about with John's health problems. He'd figure out how to deal with it on his own. He was a fucking grown man, after all, and he needed to start acting like one.

"It's nothing all that important," he responded, squeezing Conner's hand. "How's John doing?"

Conner had had to leave Lorcan to finish cleaning up the lunch dishes when he had heard the sound of John's moans from down the hall. Conner had much bigger problems than Lorcan's insecurities.

"I gave him something for the pain and a heating pad, but not before I threatened to spank his ass and made him agree to go back to the doctor."

"Wow, I'm impressed. I was beginning to think you were never going to get through to that stubborn ol' coot."

Conner laughed, but it was without his usual jubilance. He looked so worn out and scared, and that scared Lorcan. Conner rarely let things bother him for too long. He was by far the happiest man Lorcan had ever met, so this new, subdued Conner scared the shit out of him.

"How is he really?" Lorcan pressed harder.

"Not good," Conner responded quietly. "I didn't use all that much persuasion on him. I think he's finally starting to worry that something is very wrong, and I gotta tell you…." Conner's voice cracked, and he swallowed hard before continuing. "I can't lose him."

Lorcan went to his knees beside Conner and pulled him into a tight embrace. "Shh, you are not going to lose him. He'll be fine, you'll see." Lorcan wasn't so sure John would be fine, but unless told otherwise, he wouldn't let Conner give up hope. Until then, they had to believe that the doctors could treat whatever had attacked John's back and put him in bed. Conner returned the embrace, his shoulders shaking as he silently cried against Lorcan's chest, and Lorcan let go of his own worries. They seemed so insignificant compared to what Conner was dealing with. He only had to worry about how he had treated the men he loved. Conner had to worry on possibly losing the only man he'd ever loved.

CHAPTER
THREE

THE sight of someone in distress shouldn't have brought a smile to his face, but Ty couldn't help it. He was fucking giddy. The way Lorcan had clung to Quinn as they walked across the yard, his eyes wild and scanning the area—oh yeah, he'd have the man hightailing it back to Indiana by the end of the month. The thought made the smile on his face grow. *Nothing personal, pansy boy, but Quinn is mine.*

Just because he *wanted* to submit didn't make him weak. He submitted because he liked the way it made him feel, though he could easily admit that it felt pretty damn good to be the aggressor for a change. This was completely about his own pleasure, what he needed, and what he wanted. He damn sure hadn't opened up his heart to be standing in the shadows, sneaking around and watching Lorcan enjoy what was his. And Quinn *was* his.

Ty hadn't seen Lorcan return to the barn with Quinn after his little freak-out, and he spent the rest of his afternoon doing shitty jobs with a huge smile on his face. He still had a smile that nearly split his face wide open when Quinn called to him as he was heading to his truck.

"Hey, Ty, got a minute before you head home?"

Ty pushed his good feelings down below the surface and schooled his features. He'd barely let Quinn say two words to him beyond what work needed to be done, but since Lorcan would be leaving soon, he might as well let Quinn start working his way back into his good graces. Yet he didn't want to look too eager, so he leaned on the hood of his truck, going for a disinterested expression. "Sure, what's up, boss?" he asked dryly.

Quinn stepped closer, pushing his hat back a bit and wiping the sweat from his brow. Jesus, the man was hot, and not just hot from the late-afternoon Oklahoma sun either. Those bulging muscles, glistening with perspiration and flexing as he moved, were making Ty's mouth water. He couldn't help but stare, his body heating up and his cock coming to life, but he kept his face neutral.

"Clint tells me you've been asking about work on other ranches. You plan on leaving?" Quinn asked.

"Just looking for work a little closer to home. Puttin' a lot of miles on my old truck, ya know." *And just wanting to know how you'd react to me leaving.* From the look on Quinn's face, it didn't seem as if he was very happy about it.

Quinn shoved his hands into the front pockets of his jeans, his brow furrowing. "We're going to be breaking ground on the new bunkhouse next week. You're more than welcome to stay there once it's complete."

Nope, he doesn't want me to leave. It took all his will to keep the grin off his face and to stop the victory whoop that threatened to rumble up out of his chest. He'd expected Quinn to come and ask him if he had anything to do with what was happening to Lorcan, or at the very least to find out if Ty had heard any of the other hands bragging about it. Obviously, that wasn't as big of a priority as the thought of Ty leaving the ranch, and that just made the sweet fluttering in his gut feel all that much better.

"Why? Would you miss me if I left?"

"Hell yeah, I'd miss you," Quinn responded instantly. "I've been trying to get you to talk to me for weeks. If I didn't care about you, why would I have tried so hard, huh?"

Quinn had tried, but Ty hadn't been ready to hear what the man had to say, at least not while Quinn was walking around with a stupid shit-eating grin on his face and his head in the clouds. It was a daily reminder that Lorcan was getting what Ty yearned for. Not *everything* Ty longed for, like the kiss of leather or the sweet pain he knew Quinn could dole out—no, those things were still reserved for Ty. He took comfort in knowing that those things were shared only between the two of them. Lorcan wasn't part of that special side of their relationship and never would be. Yeah, since Lorcan would be packing soon, he needed to start rebuilding the communication between him and Quinn.

"I wasn't ready to hear what you had to say," he finally responded. "I was pretty pissed off, ya know?"

"I know," Quinn said sincerely. "That's why I wanted to talk to you, to apologize. Fuck, Ty, I miss being able to talk to you."

Ty shifted slightly, running a hand across his chest, the ring in his right nipple tugging and sending a tingling sensation racing down toward his hard shaft. "Talking the only thing you miss, Quinn?" he asked seductively.

Quinn's eyes went wide, and though he covered it up quickly, Ty saw the desire in those blue eyes. He was even more convinced that Lorcan wasn't fulfilling that need in Quinn. He knew personally that it was a hunger that could only be repressed for so long. Before Quinn could respond, Ty pushed himself away from the truck and headed for the cab. He knew all he needed to know for now. "Just kidding," Ty interrupted, sliding into his truck. "I gotta run. Hot date tonight, but maybe we can talk later."

"Sure," Quinn stuttered, stepping back from the truck.

As Ty pulled away from the drive, he let loose the smile he'd been holding back. Yup, Quinn was still so very much his.

AFTER Ty's hasty departure, Quinn stared at the ground long after the dust and gravel settled. "What the fuck just happened?"

He'd only wanted to talk to Ty, make sure he wasn't leaving the ranch on account of something personal. Okay, so he knew it was personal, but Ty was the only person he hadn't made amends with, and he desperately wanted to. It was Ty who had helped set him on the path to healing and helped him let go of the anger that had been crushing him after Lorcan had left. Ty, whether he knew it or not, was the main reason Quinn had become the man that could make Lorcan happy. If Ty wanted to leave, there wasn't a whole lot Quinn could do about that. It would be selfish as hell to ask the man to stay, seeing as Ty had admitted he was in love with him. However, he could at least try to salvage their friendship, and if that wasn't possible, then he wanted to at least say thank you to the man.

He'd also meant to ask if he had heard any rumors around the ranch about the message left on Lorcan's truck. He could admit that he had silently wondered if it was Ty who had done it, but the more he thought about it, the more he decided it just didn't seem like the cowboy's style. Besides, it had been weeks since Quinn had ended their physical relationship, and nothing had happened until yesterday. Hell, the man didn't even talk to him, and when his job was done, he couldn't get to his truck and leave the ranch fast enough. Nah, Ty wasn't involved, but he might have heard who was. When Ty had rubbed his hand across his muscular chest, Quinn had known the moment Ty had hit his ringed nipple from the way his breath hitched ever so slightly and his nostrils flared. In that moment he had a sudden flashback to Ty bound, screaming and begging. God, it had felt so fucking amazing to master all that strength.

Lorcan wasn't the type of man who would ever allow anyone to hit him, not even during sex, which was fine, since Quinn couldn't imagine ever raising a hand or a flogger and marring Lorcan's perfect skin. Yet as he stood in the middle of the barnyard, his body trembled with desire as the blood rushed south, straight to his prick. Images of Lorcan tied to his bed, loving every inch of his luscious body, driving Lorcan out of his head with need and lust until he was begging Quinn to allow him to come.

"That's it," he mumbled, adjusting the bulge in his jeans. "Early bedtime tonight."

He'd set the schedule in the morning so that Ty was working with him. A day of riding and checking fences with Ty would give them plenty of time to chat. Right now, he had a few fantasies to make come true.

"IT'S only eight o'clock," Lorcan protested weakly as Quinn pushed him into their room and shut the door behind them with his foot. Quinn's lips never left his neck, nor did his hands stop roaming up and down Lorcan's back.

"I didn't say we were going to sleep, just that we were going to bed." Quinn's breath tickled against Lorcan's skin as he spoke.

Good point, he thought, but he didn't say it aloud. He was too busy moaning as Quinn began kissing and sucking the sensitive flesh below his ear. He had spent the day on a crazy emotional ride, and mentally, he was exhausted. He still wasn't sure what he was going to do about the newest message, and he felt sick in his heart for Conner and John, but at the moment, he just wanted to lose himself in the bliss his lover was offering. He wanted more than anything to shut off his brain, tuck all the agony and uncertainty down and lock it away. It would still be there tomorrow, but right now, he concentrated on the pleasure as Quinn pushed him onto the bed and covered his body with his larger frame.

"Have I told you today how much I love you," Quinn murmured as he kissed his way across Lorcan's jaw.

"Yes, but I wouldn't mind a little physical reminder."

Quinn leaned back, holding himself up on his hands, and looked down at Lorcan, anticipation and heat in his blue eyes. He ground the hard bulge in his jeans against Lorcan's equally hard shaft, causing Lorcan to cry out. "This isn't physical enough?" Quinn winked, his eyes twinkling with a devilish gleam.

"I don't know," Lorcan teased back, thrusting his hips. "Not sure I can get the full effect through so many layers of clothes."

His lover hissed at the hard press of their cocks before leaning down, his tongue demanding entrance against Lorcan's lips. He opened to him, and a thick growl escaped Quinn before he dove in for a full-out possessive kiss, Lorcan giving back as good as he got until the kiss ended, leaving them both breathless.

"Still too many clothes," Lorcan complained, pulling at Quinn's T-shirt.

Quinn sat back on his haunches, straddling Lorcan's waist, and whipped off his T-shirt in one fluid movement. Fuck! The man was sexy. Quinn had always been a large man—hell, in Lorcan's opinion, larger than life. His broad chest, thick with muscle and tightening and releasing with every movement, was making Lorcan's cock swell nearly to bursting. He reached up and ran his fingers through the sparse hair on Quinn's pecs, the softness tickling his skin. He moved slowly down Quinn's body to his navel, then back up, his fingers drawn to the dark discs, teasing one nub until it was hard and erect before giving the other the same treatment.

"God, I love having your hands on me," Quinn moaned.

"My hands love being on you," Lorcan responded in a husky voice. He moved downward again, not stopping until he reached the waistband of Quinn's jeans and popped the button. "They love being on every inch of you."

Easing down the zipper, Lorcan gently released Quinn's engorged shaft and brushed a whisper of a touch along the entire length. The deep moan Lorcan pulled from his lover as he wrapped his hand firmly around the tender flesh was rewarding. Every day he learned something new about the man, and with each new discovery, his love grew until sometimes he felt as if his heart would burst out of his chest. He loved hearing how his touch gave Quinn such pleasure, loved the look in Quinn's eyes as he stared down at him with awe and tenderness swirling with lust and need in his beautiful blue eyes. More, he loved how just being near the man made Lorcan feel as if nothing else in the world mattered. Even the fact that someone seemed to have some kind of vendetta against him seemed insignificant. As Quinn leaned down and took his mouth in a sweet, tender kiss, everything except Quinn rushed from his mind. Tomorrow he'd figure out what to do about the newspaper clipping; he'd worry about Conner and John and everything else that had his head throbbing and his heart aching. Right now, he concentrated on just how perfect this moment was.

CHAPTER
FOUR

THE flex and release of thick, bulging muscles was usually enough to grab Ty's attention and send his blood rushing south. He loved broad, muscular men, even more so when said muscular men were tanned, with work-roughened hands and a dark Stetson pulled low over blue eyes, but not today.

Ty had thought it would be a good idea to give Quinn a couple of days to think about their last conversation, so he'd called off work the last two days. Maybe with a little time to let sink in what he had given up, the man would... hell, he didn't know what he expected from Quinn. Ty knew what he had *hoped* for, but he was a fucking idiot. What a fool he'd been was hammered home as he stood hidden by a large tree that overlooked a small pond, watching as Quinn pounded into Lorcan, who was bent over a large log. Ty's blood wasn't rushing anywhere; it was boiling in his veins. Even though he knew what it felt like to be on the receiving end of that powerful body and thick cock, arousal wasn't even in the running for the competing emotions currently raging through him. Anger, rage, betrayal, jealousy, envy, and a host of other negative feelings were battling for supremacy as Ty continued to stare at Quinn and Lorcan.

Each day since Lorcan had weaseled his way back into Quinn's life, Ty's anger grew just a little more. It was becoming harder and harder to keep his focus on the prize. Dammit, he couldn't afford to let his anger and jealousy make him lose focus. Ty's hands curled into fists. Watching the two of them together was enough to make his fucking head explode. His head was pounding, the contents of his stomach swirling around sickly in his nauseated gut, yet he couldn't turn away from the sight. It was torture watching his Dom, his lover, fuck someone else.

He can't give you what you want, what you need, he silently told Quinn.

Quinn's hands tenderly caressing up Lorcan's back, the gentle kisses to Lorcan's shoulders—that wasn't Quinn. Quinn liked it hard and rough. The Quinn he knew was powerful and needed an outlet for all that raw power. He needed someone who could submit to all that unharnessed strength. Someone who would take his brute force, revel in it, and beg for more. *Quinn needs me.*

That little sissy with his long girlish hair would never be enough for a man like Quinn. A pretty face and fancy hair were great to look at, but Quinn would never be happy with someone as weak as Lorcan. The man looked as if he'd cry at the first lick of Quinn's leather; the second stroke would break him. Ty just needed to be patient. Eventually Quinn would realize that Lorcan wasn't what he needed, but if Ty could send Lorcan running home to Mommy and Daddy before then, all the better. The look on Lorcan's face when he walked out and saw what Ty had left on his truck had been priceless, the scared scanning eyes after the newspaper clipping even more rewarding. At the rate it was going, and with Lorcan's history of running when he got his little feelings hurt, Ty held on to the hope he'd see Lorcan packing within the month.

"I will get him back," he vowed quietly. Nothing would stop him, certainly not someone as insignificant as Lorcan.

"Enjoying the scenery?"

Ty whirled around at the unexpected voice and came face to face with a dark-haired, dark-eyed, and smirking cowboy. Ty glanced back over his shoulder, hoping the stranger couldn't see what he'd been staring at, but there was an unobstructed view of Quinn fucking Lorcan. No chance he could play dumb. Ty's cheeks heated as he turned back to the intruder.

"Not every day you get a free porn show." Ty shrugged.

The stranger studied him, his face unreadable. Not too many cowboys were very fond of the *queer boys* in these parts, and Ty shifted his stance, his muscles tightening in anticipation. Ty wasn't the least bit intimidated and took the opportunity to do a little studying of his own. The cowboy had a couple of inches on him, but Ty made up for the height difference in the thickness of his arms and chest. The stranger was leaner, his muscles well defined, his body more like that of a sprinter compared to Ty's stocky, built-to-kick-ass frame. Not that he'd had to throw down too often, but he could hold his own when necessary. He fucking hated gay bashers, and he instinctively curled his hands into fists.

Ty's muscles relaxed slightly as the stranger smiled. They completely relaxed and he uncurled his fingers when the man said, "I hear you can at Xavier's."

"Not anymore," Ty responded with a smile of his own. "His shows are high dollar these days. Exclusive memberships only."

If the guy knew about the shows at Xavier's, a members-only club, more than likely he was batting for Ty's team. Not that he cared, but not too many people who weren't into the scene were familiar with Xavier's. That had been true even back before the place became an actual club. Jonathan Xavier, a self-made millionaire, hadn't started the club to make money, though he certainly did now. Originally, it had been a small group of men who shared a common interest, but as it grew, Jonathan had bought a nondescript warehouse on the outskirts of Jackson and turned it into one hell of a club. The best part was he was discreet and ran a high-quality club with zero advertising.

I need to see if ol' Xavier is looking for any bartenders. Maybe I can introduce Quinn to him. He was pulled from his musings when the cowboy said, "Blake Henderson," and stuck out his hand.

Ty hesitated briefly, wondering if he should give his real name. After all, he'd just been caught as a peeping tom, and he wasn't so sure he wanted Quinn to know he'd been spying on him. *Fuck it.* He shook the offered hand. "Ty Callahan."

Blake held on to his hand longer than was necessary as he nodded in the direction of where Quinn and Lorcan were. "That your boss man, or you just wandering?"

Ty pulled his hand free, schooled his features, and quickly thought of a passable lie. "Yeah, I work for him. I was heading down, thinking of taking a dip on my lunch hour, but found the place otherwise occupied."

Blake turned his attentions back to him. Dark, nearly black eyes met Ty's. "And you figured you'd stay for the show, huh?"

Ty couldn't very well deny it, so instead he just shrugged and said, "You mean to tell me you'd have come up on that"—he jerked a thumb over his shoulder without looking back—"and not enjoyed it for a bit?"

Ty wasn't about to admit that there was nothing enjoyable about the show in his eyes. The last thing he needed was for suspicion to fall on his head. Quinn and perhaps even Lorcan might already suspect that he was behind the troubles that had befallen Lorcan lately.

Blake was handsome: dark stubble on his square jaw, deep tan, and stunning dark-brown eyes. He looked to be in his late twenties, but then again, Ty had always sucked at guessing people's ages. Blake could be anywhere from his twenties to his forties, but whatever his age was, when his smile turned sly, he was fucking hot.

"I plead the fifth," Blake said sensually. Ty was sure the man had been going for innocence, but with his whiskey-smooth voice, he wasn't able to pull it off. "So shall we enjoy the rest of the show or give them their privacy?"

There was no way he'd be able to control his anger around Blake if he had to watch Quinn and Lorcan. Instead of responding to the question, he asked, "You that pric—I mean, ol' man Henderson's son?"

"Yeah, I'm the prick's son," Blake responded with a chuckle. "Though he's probably rolling in his grave that I'm telling anyone we're related."

"Well, from the shit I've heard about your ol' man, doesn't sound like he's got much right to be looking down on anyone or rolling in his grave or whatever it is he's doing now."

"My first guess is, feeling a little warmer than he did here in Oklahoma in the dead of summer." Blake pegged him with a hard glare. "You still didn't answer my question."

"I think I'll take option number two." He held out his hand once again, ready for this conversation to be over. "It was good meeting you, Blake Henderson."

Blake took the offered hand, but instead of shaking it, he gripped Ty's hand firmly, holding on. He ignored the goodbye and shocked Ty by saying, "How long have you been a submissive?"

"Excuse me?"

"I asked you how long—"

"Ain't nothing wrong with my hearing, I heard you," Ty interrupted. "What the fuck kind of question is that?"

"A simple one," the cowboy responded easily. Ty tried pulling free of the hold Blake had on his hand, but the man only held tighter. "Answer the question and I'll reward you by releasing your hand."

Ty glared at Blake and tried to pull his hand free. Blake only gripped it tighter. "Who the hell do you think you are?" he spat.

Suddenly, Blake seemed much larger than he'd appeared only moments before. He had a commanding presence, and the authoritative snap to his voice had Ty's dick twitching. He fought to keep his composure and lowered his eyes, not wanting Blake to see the struggle within them. God, it had been way too long.

"Such anger inside you." Blake's tone softened. "It's obvious that you either don't have a Dom or your Dom is not meeting your needs."

That was the understatement of the year. The man to whom he'd been submitting for the last year, the only man he wanted to submit to, was currently behind him fucking the hell out of someone else. "I don't have a Dom," he replied angrily.

Blake released Ty's hand, but Ty could feel the dark eyes boring into him. It took every bit of control he could muster not to squirm under Blake's scrutiny. After what felt like an eternity, the man finally asked quietly but confidently, "Would you like one?"

Yeah, I would. I know the perfect man for the job if you could just go and pull him off the sissy boy, Ty thought grudgingly. It had been weeks since he'd been with Quinn or anyone else for that matter. His skin felt as if it were crawling, itchy, and he was about to fucking lose it if he didn't get some release soon, but he knew what he wanted. He wanted Quinn.

The idea that this man could tell that Ty was submissive just from looking at him was intriguing. Moreover, the dark cowboy was hot, confident, but as badly as Ty wanted what the man was offering, he shook his head. "Not looking for a Dom."

Blake reached into his back pocket and pulled out his wallet. Flipping it open, he pulled out a card and held it out to Ty. "This is my number. You change your mind, and you give me a call."

Ty stared at the card briefly, then took it and stuffed it into his back pocket. "You normally go walking around in the fields looking for men to pick up?"

"Nope," he replied, returning his wallet to his pocket, watching Ty with intense brown eyes. "This would be a first, but I know what I like, what I want."

Wanting is a bitch, isn't it? He should have been flattered, but wanting something you couldn't have sucked big-time. He stiffened when he heard a loud shout that sounded a lot like "Quinn" being yelled out in the throes of passion. The anger that he'd forced to a simmering temperature in his veins when Blake walked up on him boiled over again. Ty yanked the brim of his hat further down, shielding his eyes, and stepped past Blake. "See ya around," he said gruffly.

Blake didn't respond, but Ty could feel his eyes on him as he walked stiffly away. He made it out of the small grove of trees and mounted the gelding. He was halfway across the field, well out of earshot of Blake, before he finally took a deep breath and cursed. "Fucking Lorcan, I'm beginning to seriously hate you."

THE cool water felt amazing on his heated skin as Lorcan dove into the pond. What he didn't like was the way it cleared the last of the calm from his brain, allowing thoughts of Conner, John, and Jess to come flooding back. It was easy to lose himself in Quinn, especially when the cowboy demanded Lorcan's entire focus, body and mind, as he loved him.

As he broke the surface of the water, he shook the drops from his face and took in Quinn's reclining form as the sun glistened off his damp skin. The love he had for him swelled Lorcan's heart until it ached. He'd fought with his conscience for the last two days and finally realized that if he wanted his relationship with Quinn to grow, become a solid and lasting one, he had to be completely honest. He'd made the mistake in the past of keeping shit from Quinn, and he swore he wouldn't ever do it again. *Growing up is a bitch!* Sighing, he made his way back to shore and grabbed the towel he'd left hanging on a tree branch. Quietly, he walked over to Quinn as he ran the towel over his cooled skin. *If I'm lucky, he's fallen asleep and we won't have to talk about it. I mean, why wake him up? I can always tell him tomorrow.* He was stalling and he knew it, but dammit, he didn't want to talk about all the negative shit right now. He didn't want to lose the good feelings that had settled deep within him only moments before.

Coward, another voice in his head whispered.

Sighing again, he lowered himself to the ground next to Quinn. Quinn opened his eyes, and the smile on his face made Lorcan's breath hitch. Fuck! He was seriously thinking of putting it off a while longer. He didn't want to see the beautiful smile turn into a scowl. The word *coward* flittered through his brain again. *Oh, shut the hell up!* he told the annoying voice. *I'm going to do it, but I don't have to like it, so just shut the fuck up and give me a minute.*

"Hey," Quinn said softly.

"Hey yourself," he responded. Yup, stalling.

Quinn opened his arms, and without hesitation, Lorcan took the offered invitation and laid his head on Quinn's chest. Quinn's steady heartbeat and strong arms pulling Lorcan close gave him a little more courage.

"Spill it," Quinn ordered him with a tone that broached no argument. He must have hesitated a bit too long trying to arrange his thought, because he was interrupted by Quinn's growled warning. "Lorcan."

Lorcan propped himself up on his elbow next to Quinn so he could meet his eyes. "Okay, but first you have to promise you're not going to get pissed and go all caveman when I tell you."

"I can't promise that before I know what the hell you're so freaked out about. And don't try to bullshit me; I can see it in your eyes."

Lorcan snapped his mouth shut, effectively cutting off the denial. "Then can you at least promise you won't do anything rash? That you'll at least think about what I tell you overnight?" he pleaded.

"Fine," Quinn gritted out between clenched teeth. "Christ, just tell me already so I can make plans for whose ass I'll be kicking tomorrow for putting that look on your face."

Lorcan arched a brow at him in irritation and waited for Quinn to get a clue. After what seemed like forever, Quinn finally huffed out a breath and caressed Lorcan's cheek with the tips of his fingers. "Just tell me, babe. I hate seeing the sadness in your eyes."

One last deep breath and Lorcan mustered up the courage. "A couple of days ago I thought I was losing my mind. It felt like everywhere I went someone was watching me. You know that weird prickling sensation at the back of your neck, like you can feel eyes on you, but when you turn around there is no one there?"

Quinn dropped his hand, laying it on Lorcan's hip, and nodded. "Yeah, understandable you'd experience that after what happened."

"Right…. I kept getting that feeling, and I was beginning to think I'd lost my fucking mind or developed a full-blown case of paranoia or something. And then…." Lorcan hesitated at the emotions that were beginning to swirl in Quinn's eyes and the brow that was beginning to descend into a scowl. *Crap, Quinn is going to lose it if I finish the sentence.* He had a split second to decide if he was going to lie or tell the truth. What he wished for the most was that none of this shit had happened, but no matter how hard he wished, it wasn't going away. It had happened, and the only thing to do now was decide whether he was going to be an adult or a child about it.

Even though his gut was screaming at him to keep his fool mouth shut, to just forget about it and wait for it all to blow over, his heart was screaming just as loudly, if not more so, that Quinn had the right to know. More importantly, he had the right to know that Lorcan's first thought was to run. To head to Tulsa, demand to see for himself that Jess was okay, and then run back to Mama.

His heart obviously won, because when he opened his mouth, what came out was the truth. "I think someone messed with my watch, because I was an hour early meeting you in the barn the other day. It's worked perfectly fine since then, and when I got there, someone had tacked a newspaper clipping to one of the stalls. Not just any news clipping, but the one where Jess's mangled truck was on the front page." Lorcan cringed as the hand on his hip tightened painfully. He mentally braced himself for the storm that was about to hit, but he pushed on. "Someone had written across the bottom 'At least one of you walked away.'"

Lorcan held his breath, waiting for Quinn to start screaming and cursing him for not telling him, then get up, stomp back to the ranch, and demand answers one way or another. But he did neither of those things. Instead, he grabbed Lorcan, pulling him into a tight embrace, and whispered, "God, I'm so sorry. Are you okay?"

Lorcan nodded against Quinn's chest, the lump in his throat not allowing him to form words past it. They would need to talk about how the clipping made him feel, about Jess, and he was damn sure that Quinn would be puffing up and stomping around the ranch until he got answers. But for now, he let his lover hold him and the contentment he felt when he was in Quinn's arms surround him. It made him feel all warm and fuzzy that Quinn's first reaction wasn't anger, but to think of Lorcan's feelings. *It's not so bad being an adult,* he thought, and he snuggled in deeper.

CHAPTER
FIVE

"SEEING you with your hands on all this leather and rope has me imagining some interesting scenarios," he said into the side of Ty's neck. He pushed his growing arousal against the smaller man's ass.

Ty pushed back against him, rolling his hips. "Like breaking that new gelding or maybe creating a new halter for Jeb?" he teased.

"Oh, it's about training, all right, but I was thinking more along the lines of bringing to heel a stallion I'm particularly interested in."

"Is that so?" Ty chuckled. "You're going to need more than some strips of leather and rope to bring a good stallion under control."

Quinn stood, encouraging Ty to stand, and turned him in his arms. "I'm sure I have a couple of tricks up my sleeve, not to mention"—he grabbed Ty's hips and pulled him hard against his erection—"a very sturdy prodding tool."

Ty laughed, a great happy sound, and Quinn couldn't help but kiss Ty, his laugh tickling against his lips. "You sure seem to be in a good mood today," Ty commented, still chuckling as Quinn kissed his way over to his throat.

"Of course I'm in a good mood," Quinn said against the tanned skin of Ty's neck.

Lounging back in the large claw-footed tub, the only luxury in his too-small house, Ty relived the memories of Quinn. He tipped back his beer, took a long pull, and then wiped a hand across his mouth in disgust at the now-warm brew. At one time, the images of Quinn finding him in the barn had brought the largest smile to his face. Then, in the days after Lorcan took Quinn away, the same memory brought bouts of rage and tears. Now they gave him hope. Quinn had been happy, dammit. *Happy with me.* He downed the last of his beer, sitting the empty bottle on the floor next to the tub, and grabbed the soap. He began to wash as a plan formed in his head.

The messages he'd left about Jess were not working. *Obviously, since you saw Quinn pounding into….* Fuck, no! He wasn't even going to finish that thought. He wasn't going to think about the day at the pond, God dammit! *No!* He ground his teeth and scrubbed at his skin roughly until it turned an angry red. Ty concentrated on the pressure in his jaw, his burning skin, and pushed away the blurry images that threatened to clear into real, ugly, vividly colored memories of what he'd seen. Pure fucking stubbornness and determination helped to push them back until he could slam the door on them and deadbolt it. *Thank fuck.*

The plan. Oh yeah, right. He could see now that using Jess against Lorcan wasn't going to work. It was definitely having an impact on Lorcan, but Ty needed to step up the game, add a little more pressure, so to speak. He needed something that would push Lorcan over the edge he was teetering on. Ty rinsed the soap from his red skin and tapped a finger against the side of the cast-iron tub. What else could he use against Lorcan? The pansy man was a coward—this should be easy. *Think, think, think.*

"Oh, it's about training, all right, but I was thinking more along the lines of bringing to heel a stallion I'm particularly interested in."

"That's it," Ty said excitedly, the water splashing over the edge of the tub as he sat up quickly. Lorcan had driven Quinn to The Push, but he hadn't instilled the need that was deep within Quinn. The need to dominate, to *train a stallion*, wasn't something that was brought on just because someone's feelings had been hurt or his pride wounded. No. That need had been there in Quinn all along. Lorcan had helped push that desire to the forefront through his actions, and now that it was at surface level, now that Quinn had acted on it, Ty doubted it would just quietly go away. One thing he knew for damn sure was that Lorcan would never be able to satisfy that part of Quinn.

But I can!

Brian, the sick bastard, might have introduced Ty to the scene, but that submissive trait had to have always been in him, right? Hadn't Brian only brought out Ty's need to submit, his desire to please others? The more Ty thought about it, the larger his smile grew. Two years after his *relationship* with Brian had ended, he was even more into the scene, not less.

Ty stepped out of the tub, grabbing a towel and quickly drying his body as he made his way back to his bedroom. He had some plans to set in motion. Some very delicious plans that would help him get what he wanted.

Quinn.

"HOW the hell is it that no one knows a goddamn thing?" Quinn shouted in frustration.

"I didn't say that no one knows anything," Clint responded calmly. "I said no one is admitting to it."

Quinn laid his head back against his leather desk chair and took a deep breath. His body was thrumming with anger, and his hands ached from the way they had curled into tight, white-knuckled fists. *Who the fuck is doing this?* he thought angrily. *Who has it in for Lorcan?*

He'd kept his promise to Lorcan that he wouldn't go off half-cocked and start beating the information out of the men on the ranch, but it was growing increasingly more difficult to keep that promise. He wanted answers, and he wanted them right fucking now! Someone had to pay for the uncertainty and pain they had put in Lorcan's eyes.

Quinn knew beyond a shadow of a doubt that Lorcan loved Jess and would do anything for the man. Lorcan had fought to stay at Jess's side and hadn't abandoned him after his tragic accident. Jess was the one who had pushed Lorcan away. It was Jess who had made the decision to ban Lorcan from his life. As strong as Lorcan's love was for the big, sweet man, it had been a different kind from what Quinn and Lorcan shared. Knowing that, Jess had pushed Lorcan to Quinn. Quinn had always admired the man, even more so now. He wasn't so sure he could have done the same thing and set Lorcan free, especially while scared and looking toward an uncertain future. Quinn wasn't sure why

Lorcan loved him, why he had chosen him over Jess, but he was thankful as hell he had. It made the love Lorcan gave him all the more precious, and he would do anything to be worthy of it.

Opening his eyes and taking one last deep breath, he looked up at Clint, who was looking down at him with concern-filled eyes. "Someone has to know something, dammit. No way can this shit keep happening and not one person has heard a damn thing or seen *something*."

Clint flopped down into the chair across from Quinn and removed his hat. "Eventually someone will say something. You know how these cowboys like to gossip. Hell, they're worse than those old biddies in the quilters' guild. But I'm not so sure sitting around being patient for that to happen is the way to go. Jake and I were talking, and he suggested installing some cameras around the ranch."

"Yeah?" Quinn leaned forward in his chair, his interest in the conversation renewed.

"Yeah," Clint drawled with a smile. "Jake's kid is some kind of wiz with that kind of shit. Did you know the little bastard could hack into a cell phone and eavesdrop on your text messages, all from his comfy room, with just a laptop?" Clint shook his head. "The things these kids can do nowadays are fucking scary."

"Scary, but useful," Quinn said excitedly. "What do you need from me to make this happen?"

"Just your okay," Clint responded, taking out his cell phone and flipping it open. "I'll just let Jake know and get Blay out here this afternoon."

"We won't catch who's doing this if everyone sees the kid installing cameras. Shouldn't we have him over after dark?"

Clint waved him off with a hand. "I've already thought of that. Blay will be cleaning gutters. Kill two birds with one stone."

"You are evil." Quinn laughed. "The kid hates getting his hands dirty.

"Yup." Clint winked at him.

Standing, Quinn stretched, joints popping and muscles straining. He'd been so tense, his body on high alert since the first message had been left. His first thought had been to gather Lorcan up and take a long vacation, perhaps to a secluded beach where no one knew them and they could just enjoy each other and shut out the world outside. But as tempting as it was, he knew that wasn't the answer. The problem would still be there when they got back. Best to deal with it now. Then maybe he and Lorcan could go away and celebrate.

Nodding at Clint and leaving him to his task, Quinn left the office. He grabbed his keys off the peg by the back door and stepped out onto the porch. When he scanned the area between the main house and barn, everything looked fine. Yet looks could be deceiving. There was someone hiding behind the calm and normalcy, waiting.

After one last look around and still seeing nothing out of place, Quinn headed to his truck, started the engine, and pulled out of the drive. As he drove down the lane, he continued to glance up at his rearview mirror. He saw nothing, but it was there, lurking, just the same.

The entire drive to Jess's ranch, Quinn couldn't help the way his mind kept wandering. He hated how his gut rolled and nausea threatened when he dwelled on the doubt and uncertainty he had seen in Lorcan's eyes. He especially hated how his own doubt and uncertainty had begun to weave and mesh through his brain. Lorcan had run the last time Quinn had hurt him, and that was weighing heavily on him. Lorcan had returned from Indiana a hell of a lot stronger. He'd stood by Jess when it got really tough, but would he do the same for Quinn? Would Lorcan stand and fight against what was happening now, or would he run again?

As he pulled into the drive of Jess's ranch, his heart was hammering in his chest. Then he spotted the old truck Lorcan drove parked next to the barn, and he let out a breath he'd been holding as relief filled him. After coming to a stop, he cut the engine and scrubbed a hand across his face. His hands were trembling, and he hated that he'd been scared that Lorcan would be gone. "I have to trust him," he muttered in the silence of the truck cab.

Dammit! Get a grip! Lorcan wasn't the same confused man he'd been when he had fled to Indiana. They had both done a hell of a lot of changing. They'd made plenty of mistakes, sure, but they had also learned from them, hadn't they? The one thing that remained the same, the one constant neither of them could deny, was their love for each other. It was stronger than it had ever been, and he needed to stay focused on that. He and Lorcan might be dealing with some difficult shit right now, but their love was strong. As the realization hit him, Quinn was surprised to find his heart rate slow back to its normal pace and his hands stop shaking. Nothing, and he did mean *nothing*, would ever tear them apart again. Confident in his conviction, he stepped out of the truck and went in search of his lover.

Quinn found Lorcan in the barn, and he quietly leaned against the door frame and watched as Lorcan stacked bales of hay. Christ, the man was sexy! After Jess's accident, Lorcan had lost some of the weight he'd put on while in Indiana, but it was coming back. Quinn smiled, thinking he might have something to do with that. His lover looked muscular, healthy, and happy. Quinn's body began to thrum with arousal as he continued to watch Lorcan work. He enjoyed the feeling of his shaft slowly hardening and the way his balls began to ache slightly with need. It felt good, but what he really enjoyed the most was the way his heart fluttered and the warmth spread through him at knowing Lorcan was his, would always be his.

A low rumbling growl worked its way up out of his chest, and he let it out. Lorcan jerked, startled by the sound. The momentarily wary look in his eyes was replaced by happiness and a brilliant smile spread across his beautiful face when he spotted Quinn.

"Hey, cowboy," Lorcan drawled. He dropped the bale he'd been lifting and started toward Quinn.

Quinn met him halfway, wrapping his arms around Lorcan's waist and pulling him in tight against him. "Hey yourself," he replied before placing a soft kiss on Lorcan's lips. "You almost done here?"

"Yeah, was just keeping busy till you got here." Lorcan's hands smoothed down Quinn's back as he spoke, making Quinn shudder.

"Next time, can I suggest keeping busy and being naked while waiting for me?"

Lorcan chuckled and swatted his ass. "I'll take that into consideration." Lorcan twisted out of Quinn's arms just in time to avoid the smack Quinn intended for Lorcan's tight, sassy ass.

"C'mon." Lorcan snickered at the scowl on Quinn's face, grabbed his hand, and pulled him along. "Let's grab some lunch and you can tell me about your meeting with Clint."

Quinn allowed Lorcan to pull him along but grumbled, "I'd rather talk about it naked."

Lorcan ignored his grumblings and led him into the house. They made quick work of preparing ham and cheese sandwiches, added a few chips to their plates, and grabbed a couple of sodas. With lunch ready, they settled down next to each other on the couch.

They ate in companionable silence until Lorcan finally asked, "So, what did Clint have to say?"

Quinn washed down the last of his sandwich with his soda and wiped a napkin across his mouth before responding. "No one's talking. We're both pretty sure someone will eventually, but we're not waiting."

"Meaning?" Lorcan arched a brow at him questioningly.

"Clint's arranging to have Jake's boy install cameras around the yard. See if we can catch whoever is doing this red-handed."

Lorcan shook his head, returning his half-eaten sandwich to his plate and setting it aside. "Y'all don't have to go to all that bother and expense. I'm sure it will all blow over if we just ignore it."

Quinn set his own plate aside and pulled Lorcan to him. He encouraged his lover to straddle his lap so they were face to face. Quinn reached up and cupped Lorcan's face in his hands, holding his gaze. "It's no trouble, and I'll do anything to take that sad look out of your eyes. You do know they are wrong, don't you?" Lorcan lowered his eyes and tried to turn away, but Quinn refused to let him. "You didn't abandon or walk away from Jess. You have nothing to be sorry for."

"But—"

"Lorcan, look at me," he interrupted. Lorcan hesitantly lifted his eyes and looked at Quinn questioningly. "You did everything you could for Jess. He made his choice and you made yours. Please don't start questioning those choices now. Remember you said it was fate?"

Lorcan nodded.

"Jess is where he was meant to be. He has Collin, Jack, and you watching over him." Quinn caressed Lorcan's cheeks with his thumbs. "And you're where you are meant to be, here with me. Please don't ever doubt that."

Lorcan turned his head slightly and placed a kiss to the pad of Quinn's thumb but continued to watch him with both love and sadness swirling in his warm brown eyes. "I'll never regret my choice. I love you," Lorcan said with conviction. "But I miss him. I just want to see for myself, with my own eyes, that he's okay. I have to know that he doesn't feel abandoned. I need for him to look me in the eye and tell me."

"And if he does feel abandoned?"

"Then I'll stand by him."

Quinn's heart squeezed painfully in his chest but eased again when Lorcan leaned in and kissed him tenderly before saying, "I'll sit next to his bed around the clock if that's what he needs to help him walk again and to feel complete, like any best friend would do."

Quinn took Lorcan's mouth in a deep, exploring kiss, the doubt draining away from his body as the kiss went on and on. Lorcan was his, and he put every bit of love he felt for his man into the kiss until they were both left panting for air.

"No way would I ever give those up." Lorcan chuckled as he snuggled in against Quinn's chest, nuzzling his neck.

"Good. So what's the plan?" he asked, placing a kiss to Lorcan's forehead.

"Hmm?"

"We have a plan to catch the asshole who's leaving the messages. Now we need a plan to get you in to see Jess."

THE unease Lorcan had been feeling since making the decision to try to see Jess eased. He'd been worried how Quinn would take it, frightened that his lover wouldn't understand why Lorcan needed this. He leaned back, searched Quinn's blue eyes, but only found sincerity and determination. His love for the man in front of him grew impossibly stronger. Lorcan peppered Quinn's face with kisses on his cheeks, jaw, nose, forehead, and even eyelids, repeating "thank you" over and over and over.

Quinn laughed with each kiss and held Lorcan tight. "You're welcome."

Once Quinn had been thanked properly with a kiss that had Lorcan seeing stars and struggling to catch his breath, he once again sat back and asked, "Tell me how you're going to catch the culprit. I mean, one problem at a time, right?"

Quinn smiled and encouraged Lorcan to rest his head back against his chest, playing with Lorcan's braid as he spoke. "Clint was telling me what a little computer whiz Blay is. How he could run a video feed right to his computer."

"How's he going to get cameras hooked up without anyone seeing him doing it?"

"I asked the same thing, and that's the best part." Quinn laughed, the deep sound vibrating against Lorcan's ear. "Clint is using the opportunity to get the gutters cleaned out."

Lorcan laughed as well at the thought of Blay up on a ladder getting his hands dirty. Jake had brought him to the ranch a few times, but the kid hated ranching, especially the getting dirty and sweaty part. "Have you thought about what you're going to do when you catch them?"

"Beat the fuck out of him."

Lorcan started to pull away as alarm rang through him. He didn't want Quinn getting in trouble, and if the aggressive cowboy started going around beating on people, he'd find himself in jail for sure.

Quinn refused to let him pull away, interrupting Lorcan's internal panic by saying, "Hey, I'm just kidding. I'll no doubt *want* to kick their ass, but I'll let Ed handle it."

Relaxing slightly, Lorcan quit struggling. "It may be someone you know, someone you care about."

Ty.

He didn't have any proof, but his gut was telling him it was Ty. Quinn was trying to make amends with the stocky cowboy, but Ty hadn't wanted to hear anything Quinn had to say other than what his chores for the day would be. As far as Lorcan knew, Ty hadn't accepted Quinn's apology, and although Ty had never said anything inappropriate to Lorcan, Lorcan had felt Ty staring at him on a couple of different occasions. It had always given him the same strange tingling sensation at the nape of his neck, just like when he felt eyes on him when no one was around. It was creepy as hell.

"I've thought about that. Way I see it, if they're willing to upset someone I love, then I don't want them on the ranch."

"Still going to hurt," Lorcan said quietly. Especially if Lorcan's suspicions were correct.

"Going to suck big-time, I won't deny that, but keeping my family safe and happy is more important."

There went that balloon feeling again. Lorcan's heart swelled in his chest until it felt near to bursting. He and Quinn had overcome plenty of obstacles that had been in their way. They were together, and if Lorcan had anything to say about it, they always would be. The messages and the doubt surrounding Jess were just two more obstacles that they would have to overcome, and they would. Together.

CHAPTER
SIX

THE cameras were installed, well hidden and watchful twenty-four hours a day. Hours upon hours of footage had been recorded over the last week, and nothing. There was no suspicious activity, nothing out of the ordinary, and no new messages. Until today. The cameras hadn't picked up the culprit either, since this time, the message was delivered to Jess's ranch and stuck in the mailbox far from the cameras' lenses.

Lorcan sat at the small kitchen table and stared at the flyer. It was an advertisement for The Push. Neither the bright red title, nightly drink specials, nor the large glaring man dressed in leather from head to toe could hold his attention. No, what had Lorcan's heart about to beat out of his chest and a cold bead of sweat rolling down his spine was the message scrawled across the back.

You pushed him here once. How long before he returns?

He wished this were proof positive that it was Ty behind the messages, but it wasn't. Conner had once told him about the rumors he'd heard around town about Quinn spending time at the leather bar. If Conner had heard the rumors, then Lorcan was damn sure that by the time they got to Conner's ears, the whole damn town had already heard them. There were no secrets in a town the size of Pegasus. Eventually, no matter how careful someone was, his secrets had a way of getting out.

The idea of Quinn dressed in leather, being bound and at the powerful man's mercy, excited him, but if he were completely honest, it kind of scared him as well. He wasn't into pain, didn't want to walk around on a leash or lick someone's boots. Not that he'd ever been in a leather bar, but he'd seen enough shit on the Internet that he knew that lifestyle wasn't for him. He didn't have a problem with those who did; he just knew what he liked and what he didn't. Lorcan wasn't sure it was really Quinn's style either. His lover had been uncomfortable talking about his time at The Push. In fact, Lorcan knew that Quinn was still a little ashamed of some of the harsher things he'd done after Lorcan's return to Indiana. He also knew Quinn had met Ty at the club, but he didn't know the details, and he hadn't pushed for any more information, figuring if Quinn wanted him to know more, he'd tell him.

The one thing he was sure of was that he would be sharing this newest message with his lover. Ever since they'd first talked about how they were going to try and catch who was behind the messages, his bond with Quinn had grown steadily stronger. He was positive that this unknown person was trying to break them up, to destroy what he and Quinn had, but he or she had failed. The bond between them was stronger than ever. That wasn't to say Lorcan didn't have his fleeting moments of doubt, but they didn't last. He completely believed, without the slightest bit of doubt, that he loved Quinn and Quinn, in turn, loved him. This, whatever *this* was, would not work. It would *not* destroy his relationship with Quinn.

The back door opened and shut, and in walked Quinn. It took all of a second for Quinn's smile to falter as he met Lorcan's eyes and for him to ask, "What happened now?"

How the hell did he do that? Lorcan hadn't felt upset or freaked out, so how could Quinn know something was wrong? Lorcan shrugged and held out the flyer. Quinn took it, his eyes narrowing as he read it. He then looked up at Lorcan in confusion and asked, "You want to go?"

Lorcan rolled his eyes. "Turn it over."

Quinn flipped the flyer over in his hands, and Lorcan heard a sharp intake of breath before the ripe curse. "Motherfucking bastard!"

Lorcan jumped to his feet and snatched the flyer from Quinn before he could crush it in his fist. "That's evidence. You destroy it and we won't be able to show it to Ed."

"I'm surprised you didn't rip it to shreds. This is getting fucking ridiculous," Quinn bit out angrily.

Lorcan shrugged again and set the flyer on the table before pulling Quinn into an embrace. The man was vibrating with anger, and Lorcan held him, running a soothing hand up and down Quinn's spine until the tension began to drain from the man's muscles. He continued to hold Quinn until they both seemed better under control. Then he steered Quinn to a chair and took the one next to him.

Quinn grabbed his hand and entwined their fingers. "I don't want you here alone until we catch this bastard."

"Quinn," Lorcan said softly, "I'm not going to let them scare me."

"You should be scared," Quinn said fiercely. "Whoever is doing this if obviously a psycho who has a big fucking problem with you for some reason. Right now, the messages are meant to scare, but what's next? When he sees you're not running who knows what he'll try next."

The thought had crossed Lorcan's mind, and yeah, he was a little frightened, but not enough to let them push him into hiding like a coward. "Look, Quinn. This person, for whatever reason, wants me out of the picture. Whether it's because of what happened to Jess, the fact that I'm with you, both, or simply because they don't want another *queer* boy in town, it doesn't matter. What I do know is this is their problem, not ours. I will not let this come between you and me." Lorcan squeezed Quinn's hand. "I refuse to let them run me off."

Relief was evident in Quinn's blue eyes, even above the anger and fear, as he held Lorcan's gaze. Lorcan expected his lover to argue until he agreed to an around-the-clock bodyguard, or threaten to lock him away until the threat had passed. What he hadn't expected was what came out of Quinn's mouth.

"Marry me."

Lorcan's mouth gaped open wide. He stared at Quinn as if Quinn had suddenly grown a second head. The arguments that had begun to form in his head were, *poof*, gone like dust being blown in the wind. "What?" he sputtered in shock.

"Marry me, Lorcan. Let's show this son of a bitch he can't win."

His brain finally catching up to the conversation, Lorcan shook his head. "I am not going to marry you to prove a point to this asshole. Hell, it's not even legal in Oklahoma for two men to marry."

Quinn's free hand came up, and he caressed Lorcan's cheek, his blue eyes fierce with determination. "Then marry me because you love me, because you want to spend the rest of your life with me. Who cares if the state won't recognize it? Our friends will, our families will, and more importantly, we will. Marry me because I promise to spend the rest of my life making you happy."

A strange buzzing sensation started in the pit of Lorcan's gut, and warmth spread out through his system. He had been unsure of so many things in his life, but the one thing he had never doubted was his love for Quinn. He'd tried to fight it, at times wished it would go away, and still other times it nearly drove him to his knees with guilt, but it had been a part of him since he'd met Quinn. Why? He didn't have the answers to the whys of it, and he might not completely understand how it could be so powerful, but it was. It always had been.

"Do you love me?" Quinn asked, interrupting his thoughts.

"Yes." Now that was an easy question that he didn't hesitate to answer.

"And I love you." Quinn leaned over and placed a small kiss to Lorcan's lips. "Do you want to spend the rest of your life with me?"

Ah, another easy question. "Yes!"

The hand on Lorcan's cheek slid down to his neck, further down to his chest, the slide of Quinn's hand causing Lorcan's skin to tingle and his breath to speed up. Quinn kissed him again, licking and nibbling gently at his mouth before saying, "Good, because I want to spend the rest of my life loving you."

The hand over Lorcan's heart began to massage and caress him through his T-shirt, Quinn's eyes never leaving his. They sat there for long drawn-out moments, inches apart, breathing each other in. "Marry me," Quinn whispered, his warm, sweet breath tickling against Lorcan's lips.

Before he realized what he was doing, he said, "Yes." In that moment, it was the easiest question of them all to answer.

Quinn stood, lifting Lorcan from his chair without ever losing the contact of their mouths. Quinn deepened the kiss, pushing his tongue past Lorcan's lips, kissing him with such passion that Lorcan's toes curled as his soon-to-be husband carried him to the bedroom. Even as

Quinn laid him down on the large king-size bed and covered Lorcan's body with his larger one, the kiss went on and on until Lorcan was dizzy from it. As clothes began to fall away, neither one of them spoke a word, hands seeking skin, lips to lips, blue eyes to brown, until they were both naked and pressed together skin to skin from chest to toe.

Lorcan hadn't noticed Quinn donning a condom, or coating his thick shaft with lube, he had been so focused on the love he saw in Quinn's eyes, but he was acutely aware of Quinn entering him, how perfect it felt as their bodies merged together as one. The stretch and burn gave way to pure bliss as Quinn began to slowly slide in and out of him. Wrapping his legs around Quinn's hips, his feet locked at the small of Quinn's back, Lorcan took on the same slow, steady rhythm of Quinn's pace with his hips, meeting each gentle thrust with one of his own.

They moved together in perfect sync, following a silent melody that only their bodies could hear, and all the while, they continued to stare at each other. Quinn's beautiful blue eyes, made all the more stunning by the love and desire they held, nearly robbed Lorcan of his breath. Quinn seemed to know exactly what Lorcan needed, what he was feeling. As the first telltale signs of his impending orgasm tingled at the base of his spine and his balls drew up tight against his body, Quinn's thrusts became harder, and he rolled his hips between each thrust, applying the perfect amount of pressure to Lorcan's cock pressed between their bodies.

When Quinn pressed down hard, his body going bow tight and his face slack in pleasure, Lorcan heard his name pass Quinn's lips, sounding like a prayer. The gorgeous sight of his lover lost in pleasure was enough to send Lorcan over the edge. His own release shot through him, and he cried out Quinn's name as wet heat flowed between their bodies.

Quinn lay heavily on him, a solid weight, perfect against him, and they continued to stare at each other as their heart rates and breathing returned to a more normal pace. Lorcan knew that whatever happened next—a new message, another attempt to run him off—it wouldn't work. He and Quinn would face it together.

It was fate.

CHAPTER
SEVEN

HIS skin was going to crawl right off his body and his fucking head was going to explode if he didn't get some relief soon. Weeks Ty had waited. He had tried to be patient and give Quinn time to come to his senses and realize what a mistake he'd made by letting Lorcan weasel his way back into his life. Ty paced the small confines of his living room like a caged animal, his heavily booted steps loud and angry like the beating of his heart.

"Why the fuck isn't the pansy running?" he growled to the empty room. His hands curled into tight fists as rage filled him.

He'd never been one to be violent toward others. Even when the opportunity had presented itself, rage, betrayal, and hurt consuming him, he hadn't beaten the fuck out of Brian when he found him passed out drunk. The man had just abused him the night before, had continued to beat him, fuck him, and humiliate him even after Ty had used his safe word, and still he hadn't acted on those feelings. Instead, he had gathered up his meager belongings, walked out, and followed Brian's last order of "Be gone before I wake up and don't let me ever see your pathetic ass again."

With two dollars and fifty cents in his pocket and a face swollen black and blue, he had left without retaliating, never lifting a hand to his abuser nor reporting the rape and beating to the cops. Not that the cops would have done a damn thing anyway. In their eyes, he would just be some sick little queer who liked to be tied up and whipped. Still, he should have bashed in Brian's ugly, smug face while he had the chance. At the time, the thought never even entered his mind. He had taken his broken body, wounded pride, and battered soul, and moved on. So why were his thoughts swirling and forming into dark images of beating Lorcan's way-too-pretty face to a bloody pulp?

Ty continued to pace, clenching and unclenching his fists, trying to rein in the need to cause violence that held him in its clutches. If he hadn't acted out toward Brian violently when Lord knew the man deserved it, why was the need to hurt Lorcan consuming him? The only reasoning Ty could come up with was this time his heart was fueling his revenge-filled brain. Brian had already beaten any love he'd ever felt for the brutal Dom out of him by the time Ty had left. He loved Quinn, and that had to be the difference. His love was swirling and entwining with jealousy and rage, and he was a time bomb ready to detonate.

"I need to get a fucking grip," he grunted angrily, pulling harshly at his hair, "or so help me God, I will fucking kill him!"

"Hey, Clint, is it true? Lorcan's finally going to make an honest man out of the boss man?"

Jake's words from earlier in the day and the nod of Clint's head came rushing back, and Ty's blood boiled over, turning into hot molten lava in his veins. *Lorcan will not marry Quinn. Quinn will not marry Lorcan. He's mine.* "Do you hear me, you fucking pansy bastard?" he screamed at the top of his lungs. "Quinn is mine!"

Ty snatched an empty beer bottle from the coffee table and hurled it across the room. The mirror on the far wall shattered as the bottle made contact. He stood there, his breath harsh pants as he watched a thousand shards of glass explode and fall to the floor, the sound inaudible above the roar of blood in his ears.

You're losing it, man. Get a grip. Breathe, just fucking breathe, and get your shit together before you do something really stupid. If you kill Lorcan, Quinn will never be yours. Find another way, man. Think!

Ty grasped at the last rational thought screaming at him through the haze of red-hot fury. The voice in his head was right. Though outnumbered by the voices screaming for blood, it was right, and he needed to hold on to that thought. He opened his fists and looked down at his hands where his fingernails had made half-moon impressions in the flesh of his palms. Ty watched them slowly fill with blood. *Breathe. C'mon, man, one deep breath at a time. Breathe.* "I need to find some peace," he muttered as he tried to hold on to the last of his rationality and focus on the pain in his hands. "I need some fucking calm."

It had been weeks since he'd had any peace, and he knew if he didn't find some soon, even for a moment, he'd end up doing something he'd regret. Wiping his hands on his jeans, he grabbed his keys from the counter and headed for the door. He needed The Push.

The club was busy for a Tuesday night, and Ty nodded to several familiar faces as he made his way to the bar. It wasn't as packed as it would be on a Friday or Saturday night, but there was a nice mix of subs and Doms, and he easily found himself an empty stool at the bar.

"What can I get you?" the bartender asked with a smile.

Ty didn't recognize the tall, slim man. He was cute, but Ty didn't waste his time flirting. The blond-haired stranger had "sub" written all over him. "Bottled water, and don't open it." He dropped a five on the bar.

The man rolled his eyes in disgust at Ty's request, grabbed a bottle of water from the cooler, and set it in front of Ty. "That's two fifty," he said, cocking out a hip and placing his hand on it.

Ty picked up his bottle, nodding toward the money on the bar, and ignored the man's hissy fit. Ty turned on his stool, taking in the club. He heard the bartender huff behind him and drop his change onto the bar behind him. A smile curled Ty's lips. The man wouldn't last long at The Push, not with that prissy attitude.

Caleb, a big bear of a Dom, was sitting at a small table near the front of the club watching a whipping take place on the stage. Ty had been on the receiving end of Caleb's bullwhip a couple of times in the past and knew he was a very strict and very skilled Dom. Unfortunately, Ty wouldn't be at the end of his whip tonight. A small twink dressed in tight leather shorts, with a ball gag secured around his head, was kneeling at Caleb's feet. The sub had a blissed-out look on his face as he rested his cheek against Caleb's thigh. *Yeah, Caleb's skill is still top notch, you lucky boy*. He sighed at his loss and went back to scanning the club.

On the other side of the room he spotted Johnnie Mark—yeah, that was his real fucking name as far as Ty knew. Ty opened his water bottle and took a few sips while he watched Johnnie as he spoke to Marcus, the owner of The Push. Ty had also enjoyed a couple of scenes with Johnnie in the past. The tall, muscular Dom was relatively new to the lifestyle when he had first come into the club, and Marcus had suggested Ty for the Dom's introduction. Johnnie had been clumsy, his strokes uneven, but he had the makings of a decent Dom. The man might not be his first choice, but Johnnie didn't have a sub at his feet, and Ty wasn't being fussy tonight. He just wanted a release from his throbbing head and something to soothe his itchy skin. Ty had just taken another gulp from his water and replaced the cap, intending to walk across the club and proposition Johnnie, when a deep voice to his right gripped Ty's attention.

"Still in need of a Dom, I see."

Ty's head whipped to the right, and he found himself staring into the dark, nearly black eyes of Blake Henderson. Blake studied Ty for a moment and then drawled, "Looks like you're in even worse need than the last time I saw you."

Ty's first thought was to tell the arrogant prick to fuck off, and continue with his plans to take Johnnie Mark into the back room, but for some unknown reason, he found himself hesitating.

The new guy behind the bar strolled up with swishing and swaying hips. "Hi, handsome, I'm Toby. What's your pleasure?" he asked seductively, batting his lashes at Blake.

Blake looked at the water in Ty's hand before turning his attention back to Toby. "Water's fine."

"And do you trust me to open it for you?" Toby asked snootily, tossing a nasty look in Ty's direction.

Ty just shrugged at the questioning look Blake gave him. He'd seen it enough times in the past, drugs being slipped into drinks, and he never accepted open bottles from people he didn't know. Nothing personal.

"Sure," Blake drawled, winking at Ty. He paid for his water, telling Toby, "Keep the change," before turning his attention back to Ty. "Anyone here piqued your interest yet?"

Ty gave a noncommittal shrug and opened his water bottle, taking another drink as he scanned the club once again, this time in search of

Johnnie. He sighed with disappointment and recapped his bottle when he spotted Johnnie with his arm around Drew. Ty had worked a long time with Drew. He knew he was a damn fine sub, and Johnnie would be having a damn fine time tonight. *Fuck! That could have been me being led to the back,* he grumbled silently.

"He wasn't right for you," Blake said as if he had read Ty's thoughts.

"How the hell do you know what I need or who I need it from?" Ty snarled, glaring at Blake.

Blake didn't even flinch at the venom in Ty's voice, just calmly tipped back his own bottle and drank deeply.

Ty was drawn to the tanned skin of Blake's throat as he continued to gulp down the water. His dark hair reflected the subdued lighting of the club, giving a blue cast to the dark black coloring. Blake wasn't dressed like most of the Doms in The Push, his cowboy boots and the belt around the waist of his dress slacks the only leather the man sported. His white shirt was tailored to fit across his shoulders and chest perfectly and appeared to be made of a fine silk. The cowboy didn't need leather—the way he held himself and the confident look in his eyes screamed dominant. Ty felt a tightening in his groin, and his cock began to fill as he took in the sexy man. Ty's body seemed to approve, and who was he to argue? He just needed to be taken out of his head for a while. What did he care if the Dom's name was Caleb, Johnnie, or Blake? If all went well, if he could find a little peace. Then he might be calmer in the morning, and he could concentrate on getting rid of Lorcan without the darker thoughts clouding his judgment.

Blake set his empty bottle on the bar, picked up a napkin and dabbed it against his wet lips, then turned to Ty and said, "Guess I'll have to prove it." Without waiting for a response from Ty, he yelled out to Toby, "Can I get a room key, please?"

Toby appeared and thrust a key toward Blake. "Room three," he growled.

"No!"

Two sets of eyes turned to Ty as he shouted. His breathing had sped to a painful level, and he fought to control it. He did need what

Blake was offering, but not in that room. It was petty and childish, but that room was his room with Quinn. "Any other room but that one."

They both continued to stare at him, Blake with a look of confusion and the man behind the bar with a look of hostility. He didn't care. He was *not* doing this in that fucking room.

Blake finally turned to Toby. "Can we have a different room, please?"

Ty watched as Toby stomped away, grabbed another key, and handed it to Blake, then said to Ty, "Room five okay with you, princess?"

Ty ignored the insult, rose from his barstool, and headed toward the back rooms. Blake must have followed him, because he heard Toby call out after them, "You sure you don't want a sub willing to do anything in any room?"

Ty stepped past the thick velvet curtain and nodded at the bouncer as he walked down the hall. He stood next to room five, lowered his eyes, and waited for Blake to unlock the door.

This was obviously not the man's first time in The Push, since Blake wasn't held up by the bouncer giving him a rundown of the rules for newbies. Good. The sooner they got started, the better. Blake unlocked the door and held it open for him. Ty took a few steps inside, took up the same position he'd assumed outside the room, and waited for Blake, keeping his eyes on the concrete floor, awaiting further instructions.

Blake took his time. Ty could hear the man closing and locking the door behind him. Saw the man move in and out of his peripheral vision as he examined the room. For Ty, his nerves frayed and feeling edgy, it felt as if he'd stood there for an eternity, the room eerily quiet except for Blake's sure steps. Finally, Blake came to a halt in front of him. He didn't speak, but Ty could feel the man's dark eyes boring into him, examining him as thoroughly as he had the room. Ty fought to remain still, but the anticipation, excitement, and residual rage made it difficult, and his muscles twitched involuntarily.

"What are your safe words?" Blake asked.

"I don't need to use safe words," he responded arrogantly. Not tonight, anyway. No one had pushed him to his limits in years, not even

Quinn. Hell, he didn't care if Blake beat him until he was unconscious as long as he could find some peace from the dark thoughts and Quinn's betrayal.

"You will with me, or I walk out the door and you find yourself either a stupid Dom or a reckless Dom who doesn't require them. Your choice."

Ty clenched his jaw, his muscles tensing as he battled with himself. Christ, Blake was an irritating son of a bitch. Ty's anger at Lorcan, at Quinn, and now at the man standing before him had Ty struggling to catch his breath and his heart beating out of his chest. He wanted to scream at the man, tell him to just pick up anything, use him any way he fucking wanted to, just do it now!

Making a demand of a Dom wasn't going to get him what he needed, so he grudgingly gave a curt nod of his head and bit out agitatedly, "Yellow and red."

"Yellow and red what?"

Ty bristled, his body flushing, and the twitching of his muscles increased. "Yellow and red, Sir," he said with disdain.

"That's better," Blake praised, not commenting on the anger in Ty's voice. "What brought you to The Push tonight, Ty? What is it you need?"

Quinn was the first thought that popped into his head, but Ty didn't say it out loud. Instead he answered bitterly, "You said yourself, I'm a sub, what the fuck do you think I'm here for?"

"With the disrespect you have just shown me," Blake said smoothly, "you are not here for submission, so what is it you want?"

Ty said the only other word that fluttered through his mind besides *Quinn*. "Pain."

"Ah, a pain slut. Not pleasure, not someone to dominate you, to push you, just pain." Blake slowly walked around him, his breath as steady as his steps. He didn't say another word until he was once again standing in front of Ty. "I can give you pain, but only if you submit to me. You give me what I want and I will reward you with what you need. You have your safe words, and I expect you to use them. One more thing before we begin. Do you want to be fucked?"

It had felt like an eternity since he'd had anyone touch him sexually, and his own hand was a poor substitute for what he'd had with Quinn. Ty started to say no, he didn't want to share that part of himself with anyone but Quinn. Then the images of Quinn and Lorcan flashed briefly, and his anger surged through him and he found himself answering, "Yes, Sir."

"Strip!"

Ty jerked at the loud, unexpected command, but his hand went immediately to the hem of his T-shirt, and he whipped it off in one quick movement. Tossing his shirt to the floor, he next moved his hand to the button of his jeans, but he stilled when Blake said, "Pick that up. Fold it and set it neatly on the floor."

Steaming with anger, Ty glared up at the cowboy, about to protest, when Blake's voice snapped like a whip. "Eyes down."

Without Ty giving his eyes permission to do so, they lowered to stare at the floor, and Ty picked up his T-shirt, folded it, and placed it neatly on the floor without conscious thought.

"Good man," Blake praised. "Now the rest."

Ty removed the rest of his clothing, folding his jeans and briefs and neatly laying them on top of his shirt as instructed.

It was as if a switch had been flicked inside Ty and his body followed the commands without question while his brain continued to assault him with angry images and thoughts. Ty welcomed the warm calm that began to move through his system as it tried to overpower the anger. *Please let the calm win,* he silently begged. He stood with his head down, eyes lowered respectfully, and waited for the Dom's next command.

CHAPTER
EIGHT

SINCE he'd first encountered the cowboy hiding behind a tree, spying on his neighbor and his lover, thoughts of Ty hadn't been far from Blake's mind. He had been intrigued enough that he had done something completely out of character and sought out more information about the man. Blake had gone as far as to sit in this same bar the last couple of nights, hoping to see Ty again. He'd shared a few drinks with Marcus Damon and found out that Ty had once worked for him and was at one time a very popular sub, but not much more. Mr. Damon protected his customers and his employees' privacy, a trait Blake admired. He'd tried to find out who Ty's former Doms were, but again he'd come up empty-handed. No matter. He had the man before him now, naked, head bowed, and it no longer mattered whom Ty had submitted to in the past, only to whom he would submit in the future.

"Clasp your hands behind your back and stand straighter," Blake ordered. He waited until Ty followed his command, then once again slowly began to circle the man who, for reasons he didn't fully understand, affected him so strongly.

Neither Ty's longish blond hair, pale-blue eyes, broad, muscular chest, or short stature were physical attributes Blake had ever found appealing. He liked his men tall, slight of build, with dark hair and eyes; obedient. The surly Ty Callahan was none of these things. As Blake studied the man before him, his arousal ignited into a delectable burn, and he couldn't help but question his strange reaction. *What is it about him?* he mused. *Why him?* He hadn't had a sub, hadn't wanted a sub, in over two years, not since....

Blake shuddered as ice-cold tendrils of grief began to slither along his spine. No, he wasn't going to think about his beautiful boy being violently ripped from his life, and he forcefully pushed away the thoughts before they could fully form. He focused on the here and now and why he was with someone like Ty.

The light glinted off the gold rings in Ty's nipples, drawing Blake's attention. Another thing he had never found attractive, yet on Ty they not only appealed to him, but he had a strong urge to reach out and tug the small rings. To feel them against his tongue as he sucked first one, then the other pierced nipple into his mouth. Forcing his eyes away from the gold rings, Blake continued his *appraisal*, moving in sure, confident steps, touching Ty randomly. The creamy globe of one taut ass cheek, a bulging bicep, and the defined muscles of a tight, flat stomach. He smiled to himself as he ran the tip of one finger down the length of Ty's thick cock and listened to the sharp intake of breath his touch elicited.

No, nothing about Ty was what he sought out in a lover, yet here he was, not only in a club he normally wouldn't step foot into but also achingly hard and struggling to keep his lust under control. Blake finally came to a stop in front of Ty. He could hear the man's quick but even breaths, and the muscles of his shoulders seemed loose. Ty appeared to be an overall study in calmness, but Blake could sense a storm brewing just below the surface of tanned skin and thick muscles.

"Bend over, keeping your back and legs straight, and grab the backs of your knees."

Ty complied immediately, this time without the slightest hesitation.

Blake knew Ty was a natural submissive, had seen it in the man the first time he'd met him in the field, but Ty was fighting against his nature. He suspected the anger that colored the man's skin and made him lash out with a venom-filled voice stemmed not only from fighting himself but from what others had inflicted upon Ty. Heartbreak, pain, betrayal, abuse—they were all there in the wariness in Ty's eyes, the protective way he put on a cocky façade, and in the pitch of his voice.

Blake didn't move to touch Ty, nor did he speak. He clasped his hands behind his back and watched Ty, knowing the humiliating position would make Ty feel vulnerable, and if he were forced to hold the position long enough, it would give Ty a small measure of the pain he was seeking. Therefore, he waited. Standing in the silent room, he waited for the stretch of tendons and muscles to ache. He waited until the ache turned into a burn and finally pain.

After long drawn-out moments, Blake reached out a hand and gently ran his fingers through Ty's blond hair. The man flinched and pulled away slightly from his touch. Sighing to himself, Blake clasped his hands once again behind his back, spread his feet slightly farther apart into a more comfortable position, and waited.

Blake wanted to ask Ty who had abused him, who had betrayed his trust, had hurt him so badly, but he doubted Ty would tell him, and no amount of force or pain would get the answers. Ty had to trust him before he would give up such secrets, and Blake wanted to know those secrets as much as he wanted Ty to submit to him. *And why this man calls to you, don't forget that mystery.*

Because he needs me, another voice in his head whispered the answer.

Blake stared down at Ty, willing the man to give up a few of the answers to the questions in his head. *Why you, Ty? What is it about you that's strong enough to bring me here?* His only response was the jerk of a muscle in Ty's powerful back and a slight increase in the man's breathing, nothing more. After thirty minutes, Ty still hadn't been able to calm himself completely, nor was he moving above the pain but muscling his way through it by pure stubbornness. The pain from the position he was in had to be increasing, but Ty didn't give in to the pain, didn't welcome it. His skin flushed a deep hue, and the anger rolling off the man was so thick in the air it was nearly palpable. Ty was not focusing on Blake. In fact, Blake wasn't so sure Ty was mentally in the room anymore. Someone else was the object of all that rage.

"Stand up and get dressed," Blake ordered, trying his best to keep the disappointment out of his voice.

Ty glared up at him shortly, then stood with a wince and grabbed his clothes. "What the fuck?" Ty snarled.

Blake ignored the question, waiting until the man was once again dressed before saying calmly, "Do you still have the card I gave you?"

"No... maybe... I don't fucking know, why?" Ty growled, a deep scowl on his face and his large arms crossed over his chest.

"When you're ready to set aside whoever it is you're thinking about, be respectful, and submit to me, give me a call." And with that, Blake walked to the door, opened it, and strolled down the hall without another word or a glance back.

Blake's body was cursing him as he made his way out of The Push, his aching shaft begging him to turn around and take his pleasure in Ty's body, but he couldn't. As badly as he wanted Ty, he refused to have a sub who wasn't focused on what they were doing together. Blake had no doubt that both he and Ty could have easily reached orgasm together. He was even more confident that he could force Ty to submit, sure in his ability to send the man flying, but he refused to force Ty. A forced scene wouldn't fulfill the need that both of them had. Afterward they would be left unsatisfied and Blake would be no closer to getting the answers he so desperately wanted from Ty.

As Blake pulled out of the parking lot of The Push, he glanced back at the club through his rearview mirror. He didn't see Ty come out the door, and he briefly toyed with the idea of going back in and making sure Ty was okay, but the urge passed, and he turned back to the road ahead of him. Hopefully he would be hearing from the stubborn cowboy in the very near future. He could be patient for a little while longer, since something in his gut was telling him that he would be hearing from Ty. His gut was rarely wrong.

"NO GOOD, rotten, arrogant son of a bitch," Ty cursed, staring at the open door. Heat raced over his body as if a lit match had been set to his skin, engulfing him in flames. The intensity of it left him shaking so hard it was surprising that his legs could hold him upright. Ty wrapped his arms around his chest in an attempt to keep from shaking apart. Who did Blake Henderson think he was? "Fucker! You don't know me," he roared, his voice echoing off the walls of the empty room. "You think you're the first person to walk away from me?" he bellowed. The full weight of that statement slammed into Ty, and his arms were no longer strong enough to keep him from shattering as his past came flooding back like a tidal wave.

Suddenly Ty was six years old.

"Where are we going?" he asked the lady with the clipboard. He was so scared of the stranger. She smiled at him, but he didn't like her smile. Her red eyes and really wrinkly skin were creepy.

"I'm taking you to your new home," she answered flatly as she buckled Ty into the back of her car.

"But I don't want a new home, I like this one," he cried. Hot tears rolled down his cheeks, and he couldn't catch his breath. Ty hadn't been at this house very long, but he liked it better than the last house he had lived at. The people here had lots of cats, and even though it was stinky and lots of times he was hungry, he liked the cats, especially the new kittens.

The lady with the clipboard ignored him and took him to a new house.

The memory faded, and in the blink of an eye, he was eight.

Looking out the window of Mr. Granger's truck, Ty took in the big building with big stairs and lots of people walking in front of it. It kind of looked like the palace in the movie he'd seen called Hercules, with the big stones holding up the roof. "Mr. Granger, this is a funny-looking feed store. It don't look nothing like the place we got the food for the chickens."

"That's because this is a special store," Mr. Granger answered.

Ty held Mr. Granger's hand as they walked up the steps, his excitement turning to dread when Mr. Granger opened the door and Ty saw the lady with the clipboard. It didn't matter how much he cried, screamed, and kicked. The lady with the clipboard and some of the other people with her grabbed him and made him stay with them while Mr. Granger walked away. He never saw the man or the little chicken he had named Charlie again.

Without the chance to catch his breath, he was twelve.

"I'm not going back!" He wasn't, he was so not going back to that shithole.

"Do you want to end up in jail, Ty? You can't keep running away or the judge will send you to juvie again," the new social worker threatened.

Yeah, well, he wasn't scared of juvie. "I don't care! I'd rather die than go back there." Ty tried to open the back door to the car, but it wouldn't budge, and the window wouldn't go down. "I'll just run away again if you take me back. Mrs. Lutz keeps hitting me when the little kids cry. I try to keep them from crying, but I can't. They're hungry, and I keep telling her they wouldn't cry if she would just feed them, but she won't listen. Then she just hits me again for being lippy."

"Ty, you have to stop making up these tall tales. Mrs. Lutz was good enough to take you in and give you a home. The cupboards are well stocked, and to be honest, Ty, it's hard to believe you when the officers walk in and everyone is sitting down around the dinner table eating. Now who do you think we would believe, you or our own eyes?"

The answer was clear as he stood watching the new social worker drive away while Mrs. Lutz stood next to him, her arm around his shoulder and her fingernails digging into his flesh.

Even the tears pouring down his face couldn't stop the next image.

"What else can I do, Ty? You refused the group home we arranged for you," Mrs. Kline said tiredly.

"You can tell me where I can find a place to live for fifty dollars," he responded angrily, waving the money she had given him at her. "How am I going to finish school without somewhere to live? I only have two months left before I graduate!"

"The group home will—"

"I'm not going to a goddamn group home! Why the hell can't I stay with Mr. and Mrs. Johnson? I have never once been in trouble while I've been there."

"Ty." Mrs. Kline sighed, pushing an envelope across her desk toward him. "I told you, you're an adult now. The Johnsons' had an opportunity to take in a younger child, but they were already at their max."

"So I'm out and the new kid gets my bed?" he asked incredulously. "They couldn't wait two fucking months?"

"I'm sorry, there is—"

"Nothing you can do," he interrupted bitterly.

Just like that, Ty found himself standing out front of Child Protective Services, homeless, with fifty dollars in his pocket. Happy fucking birthday.

When the memories finally subsided, Ty found himself on his knees, his cheeks damp with tears and his head throbbing. Scrubbing a hand across his face, he pulled himself to his feet and stood on shaking legs. He was unaware of how long he'd been held by the past. He only knew it had been long enough to leave him feeling raw and drained. With the last of his strength, he made it out of The Push, and somehow, without knowing how, he made it home.

The night hadn't turned out as he had hoped, but as he pulled back the covers and crawled into bed, his last conscious thought was that the night hadn't been a complete waste of time. In the morning, he would come up with a new plan to run Lorcan off without the darker thoughts impeding his judgment. He had a new outlet for his rage. Instead of Lorcan, Blake Henderson was now the target of his fury.

CHAPTER
NINE

THE scents of brown sugar, cinnamon, yeast, and freshly brewed coffee filled the small kitchen at Whispering Pines Ranch. Lorcan sat next to Quinn across the table from Conner, who was looking at him expectantly. Lorcan took his time and licked the last traces of Conner's sweet bread from his fingers.

"How soon before John's test results are back?" he asked Conner in another attempt to draw things out further.

Conner swatted at Lorcan playfully with a mock scowl on his face. "I already told you, it may be weeks before they have all the tests scheduled and the results back."

Lorcan nodded and entwined his fingers with those on the hand Quinn had resting on Lorcan's thigh. Conner had already told him that John's initial tests had come back looking good, and so far the doctors didn't have any reason to think it was anything life-threatening. John had been set up with a TENS unit, some crazy contraption that had something to do with shock treatments. Lorcan didn't completely understand exactly how it worked, but John was taking less pain medication and moving at least a little more, and some of the worry had eased from Conner's eyes. He'd thought shock treatments were something they used to torture mental patients in the old days, but apparently they were used for muscles as well. Didn't matter—he didn't need to understand it. Lorcan was just grateful that it appeared to be working.

"And when is John's next appointment?" Lorcan knew it was next Tuesday, but he loved teasing Conner.

"I have already told you everything I know," Conner huffed. "I've made sweet bread, brewed coffee, heard about your latest run-in with Bunny, and watched your disgusting table manners." Conner threw a napkin at Lorcan, who caught it easily. "Now will you tell me what it is you want to tell me?"

"Maybe we should pour a fresh cup—"

Quinn chuckled and grabbed the fork from Conner with his free hand just as the ol' coot lifted it in a threatening manner. "You better tell him," Quinn encouraged. "Don't know if I'll be able to protect you against this feisty thing."

"That's right," Conner agreed, bending a delicate arm and flexing. "Unless you want me to unleash all this on you." The small snicker escaping Conner as he spoke did nothing to help make him menacing.

"Okay, okay. Simmer down, Rocky," Lorcan laughed. "We were just wondering if, in your busy schedule, you might fit in attending a wedding."

Conner looked back and forth between Lorcan and Quinn and then let out a squeal that left Lorcan's ears ringing. Lorcan never would have believed that Conner could move so quickly, but he was out of his seat and pulling both Quinn and Lorcan into a quick group hug before racing for his phonebook, paper, and pen faster than Lorcan could blink.

"Oh my God! When? I have so much to do. Wonder if Mrs. Church's rheumatoid arthritis is still giving her fits. I'm going to need her help in the kitchen."

"I think he might squeeze us in." Quinn beamed and pulled Lorcan against his side.

"You think?" Lorcan teased, his own smile just as wide as his lover's was.

"Oh what a perfect time for a wedding, the trees are starting to hit their peak colors; the black-eyed Susans look wonderful and should for a while yet. We may have to order a few accent flowers for the tables. I'd hate to take too many of them out of the gardens and ruin how full and beautiful they are. Have you called your mom and dad?"

Lorcan continued to stare at Quinn with a silly smile on his face. "Not yet, Conner. I will shortly."

"Oh, Caroline is going to be so excited. I hope they can find someone to run the ranch on such short notice. Lenn better not give me any crap excuse that he needs to stay back and make sure the ranch is running properly while Matthew is away. That boy needs to take it easy once in a while...."

Quinn took Lorcan's face in his hands. "You have made him a very happy man," he murmured before placing a tender kiss against Lorcan's lips. "Not as happy as you've made me, but a close second."

"That would be you in second place," he teased, returning the kiss. "I'm pretty sure I got the happiest title wrapped up."

"Kenny Marshall would be perfect for DJ. He just got a whole new lighting system. Connie heard from Joyce that he doesn't just play that newfangled music, but a nice mix. Who do you want doing your photos?"

"I trust your judgment," Quinn said to Conner, but he kept his eyes on Lorcan. Not that Conner really needed Quinn to answer; he had already moved past photographers and on to the cake, debating the pros and cons of the two local bakeries. To Lorcan, Quinn said, "When did you get so sappy?"

"Me? Oh no, you're the one that has turned into a complete sap. You're losing your tough, arrogant rancher reputation."

"Please. I'm a stone-cold hard-ass," Quinn said gruffly, his brow furrowing into his signature scowl. "Just ask any of the hands, they'll tell ya."

Lorcan kissed the scowl away. "Sorry, cowboy. I doubt any of them would describe you as tough after they heard about the candlelight dinner you set up in the barn last night. I know they won't once they hear about the rose petals you spread across our—"

Quinn shut him up before he could finish his sentence. Not that Lorcan was complaining, not with the way Quinn's tongue was pushing past his lips, demanding entrance. The possessive and thorough kiss deepened until even Conner's ranting about menu options and tuxedos became a low background buzz of noise. Lorcan's soul focus was on his sappy future husband and how he was making Lorcan's toes curl and his eyes roll back in his head.

"WELL, I'll be damned. Blake Henderson, how the hell are you?" Quinn greeted him as he stepped out of his truck with his hand extended.

"I'm good," Blake responded, taking the offered hand and shaking it. "Heard you've been having some trouble with a stalker and stopped in to see if you needed any help."

"Good ol' Pegasus rumor mill." Quinn chuckled. "I'm surprised the town hasn't solved my little mystery, had the culprit tried, convicted, and hung up by his toes down at town hall."

"Give 'em a little more time, I'm sure they'll get the bastard. So last I heard Lorcan had some trouble at Jess's place?" Blake inquired.

"Nah, just someone left a flyer in the mailbox, but we haven't had any more messages in the last week or so. Not sure if it's someone loyal to Jess, pissed off at me, pissed off at Lorcan, or just a nut job, but we're keeping a close eye on things here."

"And on your man, no doubt?"

"You know it." Quinn laughed. "C'mon up to the house and I'll pour us some sweet tea."

"Tea would be great, thanks." He followed Quinn up to the back porch, taking a seat in one of the old rockers.

"How's it going over at your place?" Quinn asked, pouring a glass of tea from the pitcher on the small table and handing one to Blake.

"Thanks," he said, taking the offered drink. "Things are pretty good from what the bookkeeper is telling me, not that I have a whole lot to do with it. My foreman is the real boss. I just do what he tells me and try to stay out of everyone's way."

Quinn brought his own tea over and took the rocker next to him. "I heard you hired Jeremy Trudell. Damn fine foreman, he'll do ya right."

Back when Blake had first taken over his daddy's ranch, one of the first things he had done was settle with Quinn. The old prick hadn't done right by Quinn, stealing all his hands, spreading nasty rumors, and nearly killing the man, not to mention his partner. A year ago, Blake wouldn't have shown up here to offer his help, and no way in hell would he have been sitting on the man's back porch sharing a glass of tea. He had known even back then, thanks to the Pegasus rumor mill, that Quinn's nasty disposition wasn't anything personal, and he knew Quinn had appreciated the out-of-court settlement after Blake's dad died. Quinn had been dealing with a bad break-up and coming out of the closet for the first time. But over the last few months, Blake had seen a huge change in his neighbor. Where before Quinn had ignored him on the few occasions he'd seen him in town—or, if Blake was lucky, had growled "hello"—now Quinn went out of his way to be friendly whenever they ran into each other. In fact, it had been Quinn who had recommended Jeremy as a foreman.

"You were right about him. He's a great guy, and thank God too. I'm not so sure the ranch would still be worth a damn if I had to be the one mucking stalls and feeding animals."

"Damn city boys." Quinn chuckled goodheartedly.

"So, there's a new rumor running around the mill." Blake arched a brow toward Quinn. "Any truth to it?"

Quinn took a large gulp from his tea, his cheeks turning pink. "If it's the one about me turning into a sap and staging romantic candlelit dinners in my barn, I plead the fifth."

"Nah, the way you walk around like you're floating on a cloud and have that stupid I-am-so-fucking-in-love smile on your face when you're with Lorcan, I knew that one was true. I'm talking about you two tying the knot." Blake already knew that one was true too—he had been standing in the bakery when Conner called and asked about a wedding cake—but it had given him a good excuse to stop by, and if he just happened to run into the stubborn Ty Callahan, all the better.

"Christ, that mill is fast. I just told Conner an hour ago. And just so you know, I don't walk on clouds." His smile turned sly. "But I might be on my wedding night."

Blake raised his glass and clinked it against Quinn's. "Congrats."

"Thanks. I haven't a clue what the hell is going on, but knowing Conner, he'll insist that the entire town shows up, so I'm sure you'll be getting an invite."

"I'll be there."

"Hey, Ty!" Quinn suddenly yelled out, waving a hand. "Did Clint tell you I wanted to speak to you?" He turned to Blake and said, "Sorry, I just need to set up a meeting with one of the hands."

"Sure," Blake said absently, his attention already focused on the stocky cowboy stepping out of the barn. He'd been waiting for Ty's call. When he hadn't received one, he'd found himself, on more than one occasion, picking up the phone, ready to call the Whispering Pines Ranch to get a phone number or an address for Ty. Luckily, he'd been able to talk himself out of it before he finished dialing the number. It wouldn't look good for him to appear too eager, but beneath his patient exterior, he was very eager to get his hands on Ty Callahan.

"Yeah, he told me. I'm busy, what do you want?" Ty yelled back, stopping in his tracks.

Blake heard Quinn sigh heavily before responding, "I just want to talk to you for a minute."

"Like I said, I'm busy. Just give my chore list to Clint," Ty snarled. He turned and headed toward the trucks parked at the end of the barn.

"It's not about work."

Ty's steps faltered for a minute, and then he moved quicker, screaming, "I'm not fucking interested!"

"Ty, stop!" Quinn roared. Then he turned to Blake and said as he rose from his chair, "Sorry, I got to talk to him, I'll be right back."

Blake noticed that Ty had stopped, but even from this distance, he could see the man shaking with anger. "It's okay. I gotta get back home anyway. Just wanted to stop by and congratulate you."

"Thanks, Blake. Stop by anytime."

"Will do." He followed Quinn down the steps toward Ty, thinking, *I can ease that anger, Ty. Just pick up the phone and call me. Better yet, let me take you home with me right now.* With each step closer to Ty, his arousal grew, heating his body as his blood made a mad dash to his groin. He knew the moment Ty recognized him by the way his pale-blue eyes grew wider and the compact body tensed even further. "Ty," he said in acknowledgement, and he tipped his hat in Ty's direction.

Blake had planned to keep walking toward his truck and let Quinn say whatever it was he needed to say to Ty in private. He'd find another way to talk to the man later, but Ty's barely audible "Fuck you" had him stopping and meeting the cowboy's glare.

He let his gaze wander appreciatively down Ty's muscular frame and back up to meet his eyes. "Hear out what Quinn has to say, and when you're done, give me a call. I'll see what I can do to make that a reality." This time he tipped his hat in Quinn's direction. "Quinn." He left them both standing with their mouths gaping open, staring like deer in the headlights, and walked to his truck.

They were both still staring at him as he started his truck and pulled out of the drive. Once he turned onto the main road, heading toward his ranch, Blake started to laugh. He knew Ty had no desire to top him. The man was a natural submissive, and although he talked tough and full of anger, beneath it all, he had a strong need to please. Blake had no doubt he could give Ty what he really wanted. With a little patience, he was absolutely sure he could bend the strong-willed Ty Callahan. He'd witnessed the way Ty reacted to Quinn and Lorcan making love near the pond, and he'd seen the anger swimming in Ty's eyes when he tried to act nonchalantly while talking about the scene unfolding behind him. Blake could practically feel the heat of raw fury, simmering just below the surface of Ty's calm exterior, a rage that was close to boiling over as evidenced by the way Ty trembled slightly and how he couldn't hold Blake's stare. The anger he witnessed that day would only explode when Ty learned about Quinn and Lorcan's upcoming nuptials. Ty's anger would rocket off the charts and explode. Ty was going to need an outlet for all the fury, and Blake had the perfect solution. He just hoped the angry cowboy didn't make him wait too long.

As it turned out, Blake's wait wasn't nearly as long as he'd thought it would be. He was stretched out on his bed shortly before midnight, watching old reruns of a crime show, when he was interrupted by the sound of his cell phone vibrating against the bedside table. Picking it up, he smiled when he saw "unknown caller" displayed across the small screen.

Blake flipped open his phone and drawled seductively, "Hello, Ty."

There was a slight pause before Ty spoke. "Uh, hi," came the hesitant reply. "Not calling at a bad time, am I?"

"No, not at all. Was just lying here watching bad acting."

"Yeah, okay... good."

The silence stretched out, and Blake waited for Ty to say more, but there was only a continued silence. "Ty? You still there?"

"Uh, yeah." A heavy breath sounded through the phone before Ty asked, "Look, I'm calling about your offer."

Blake was glad he didn't have to control the large smile on his face. "You're ready to submit to me?" he asked, keeping his voice neutral.

"Fuck, no!" Ty snarled. "I was talking about your offer from earlier today. You said you'd see about making it a reality."

"Ah, that offer. Just as well, since the tone of your voice is full of anger and disrespect." *It won't be there for long.*

"You know what? Never mind, sorry I called."

"Ty," Blake said quickly before the man had a chance to hang up.

"What!"

"Your place or mine?"

CHAPTER
TEN

WITH Quinn's last words to him—*"I care about you, but I'm in love with Lorcan,"*—still ringing in his ears, Ty had picked up the phone and called Blake. Now, as he drove toward the man's home, he wasn't so sure he'd done the right thing. It had seemed like the perfect solution at the time. Blake was sexy and willing, and Ty had called him not out of any real desire to be with Blake but instead to get back at Quinn. Had Blake still been at the farm, Ty probably would have used him. His first thought had been to lash out and punish Quinn after hearing about his and Lorcan's upcoming wedding. No doubt he would have fucked Blake through the wall of the barn right in front of Quinn had he been offered the opportunity at that moment. But now, as he drove the dark roads toward Blake's ranch, he wasn't so sure.

The truck rolled to a stop in front of the entrance to the Circle H Ranch. The large wrought iron archway, with the name of the ranch entwined with vines, looked welcoming in the headlights of his truck, but the queasy feeling in his gut wasn't so pleasing. What the hell was he doing here? His body was as full of anger as his head was with thoughts of Quinn. Even if he wanted to submit to Blake, he had some serious doubts he'd be able to be respectful, and no way in hell could he set aside thoughts of Quinn. The other problem with being here was the thought of fucking Blake held zero appeal for Ty. He had tried it a couple of times when he was younger, but he was always too nervous and too self-conscious. If he'd been a nervous wreck back when he was still an experimenting teen, he'd be a fucking basket case trying to top someone as confident as Blake Henderson. He looked up at the arch again and grimaced. He was already here. He'd probably gotten the man out of bed. The least Ty could do was show up. He'd have one beer, apologize, and get the hell out of there and home within the hour.

The light was blazing from the front windows of Blake's large log post and beam home. It reminded Ty of those fancy lodges he'd seen on a website once. Ty could fit three, maybe four houses the size of his into Blake's rustic palace.

"I was out of my league with Quinn. But this...." Ty waved a hand frantically at the house. "This is so beyond my league, like beyond the fucking stars out of my league." He was just about to put his truck in gear and slink off to his little shithole of a house where he belonged when Blake stepped out onto the porch and waved. The cowboy stood in a pair of navy sleep pants hanging loosely on his lean hips and a plain white T-shirt that appeared to be a size too small, showing off the toned chest and abs beneath. For the first time, Blake was without his Stetson, and his hair was thick and wavy and made the man impossibly sexier. *Yeah, with that sexy son of a bitch standing on the front porch, there are no words to describe how far out of my league this is.* Ty rolled down his window and leaned out. "Hey, Blake, sorry to keep you waiting. I'm just going to go now." He gave Blake a pathetic wave.

"Ty, get out of the truck," Blake called out, his voice deep. Blake, who only seconds ago had stood casually waiting, now crossed his arms over his chest and had a commanding presence about him, one Ty couldn't ignore, and he stepped out of the truck as instructed.

Ty gave Blake a sheepish smile as he stepped up on the porch. His anger had diminished, and now he just felt pathetic and wanted to go home, grab a bottle of whiskey, and have a pity party for one. "I'm just going to go."

"In the house, Ty," Blake drawled, holding open the screen door.

Ty hesitated, trying to decide if he should turn his back on Blake and make a mad dash for his truck. Sure, Blake's legs were long and he could probably catch him before he made it to his truck, but the element of surprise might make up for the difference in their strides.

"Now!"

"Pushy bastard," Ty muttered, and he stepped into the house.

The inside was even more impressive than the exterior. Rustic log posts and beams throughout the great room were impressive, but the back wall, made up completely of windows that looked out to a stunning view of the fields beyond, was even more impressive. The massive and heavy leather furniture was rugged and masculine like its owner. The main color of the room was different tones of browns but accented with intense blues, beautiful reds, and bright yellows and oranges. Ty had seen houses like this in magazines and in movies but had never been inside one. *What the hell is your white trash ass doing here? Get back in your truck and take your sorry ass home before you embarrass yourself.*

"Can I offer you a drink?" Blake asked, interrupting Ty's internal self-deprecating rant. "Or would you rather skip drinks and move right on to the reality?"

Ty shook his head. "I mean, yeah. I'll take something to drink," he stammered, toeing off his boots. Ty started to leave them where they had fallen on the rug, then remembered how Blake had reacted when Ty had thrown his shirt on the floor of the club. Bending over, he picked up his boots and set them neatly next to the door. "Whiskey, if you have it."

"I have soda, juice, and water. Or I can put on a pot of coffee if you prefer," Blake offered.

"I'm having a shit day," Ty complained, following Blake toward the kitchen area. "I could really use something a little stronger than juice or soda."

"Sorry," Blake said, opening the fridge. "I don't drink alcohol, and I got rid of the old man's stock."

"Just fucking great," Ty grumbled under his breath. "Soda is fine."

Blake grabbed two bottles of Coke out of the fridge, handing one to Ty and leaning back against the counter. He opened his soda, taking a long drink before turning to Ty and saying, "Your shit day have anything to do with Quinn and Lorcan's wedding?"

Ty nearly choked on his mouthful of Coke. "No! What gave you that idea?"

"I took you for cocky, a little high strung, and at times disrespectful, but never pegged you as a liar."

"Fuck you," Ty growled, slamming his bottle on the counter.

"We've already established that's why you're here," Blake said calmly and took another small sip from his Coke. "It was a simple question, but your response was enough of an answer. Would you like an outlet for all that anger?"

"Yeah, I would. Lucky for me I know the perfect solution." Cheap whiskey wasn't actually the perfect solution, and the hangover in the morning was going to be a bitch. But he figured it was a small price to pay to drown out Quinn's words for a few hours. He'd only taken a few steps toward the door when he was spun around and pushed up against the kitchen counter, his wrists restrained in Blake's hands. Ty's heart pounded in his chest, and his breath sped up just a little as he tried to catch up to the unexpected position change. Ty swallowed and tried to pull away from Blake's grasp, but he held tight. "What the fuck?"

"Alcohol won't help, but I can," Blake said smoothly. The confidence in his eyes appeared to be unquestionable. "I can relieve you of the pounding in your head, the tension in your muscles, and take that hurt look out of your eyes." Blake's gaze traveled down Ty's body, a small smile teasing the cowboy's lips; then he looked into Ty's eyes for a long, intense moment that Ty felt deep inside him. "I can turn all that anger into pleasure and take you out of your body." The tip of Blake's tongue teased his lower lip. "Send you soaring above it."

Ty pulled against Blake's restraining hands, his cock hardening instantly with his halfhearted attempt to free himself. To be taken out of his head, above his body, was something he wanted—no, *needed* so achingly bad. How long had it been since he'd truly felt any peace? Surely not since Quinn had returned to Lorcan. Ty groaned as Quinn's betrayal came surging back in a rush, and his stomach rolled. *Goddamn you, Quinn! What the hell have you done to me?*

Blake's thumbs caressed the insides of his wrists, tickling at the sensitive skin, bringing Ty's attention back to the man holding him. "Let him go, Ty," Blake whispered quietly. "You know you want to. You want what I'm offering. What I can give you." Blake's grip tightened to an almost painful level, a small moan escaping Ty with the pressure. "Focus on nothing but me, Ty."

TY BLINKED and stopped struggling to pull free. Blake could see the discord in Ty's eyes and added a little more pressure to the wrists in his hands, pulling another small sound of pleasure from Ty's parted lips. The last time he had had Ty before him, the man had been so consumed with rage that Blake hadn't been sure he could chisel past all that anger and had given Ty the opportunity to try to calm himself. This time, he'd help the hurting man find his calm. Where before there had only been anger in the pale-blue eyes, now they were infused with despair. The man was teetering on the edge of being completely broken by his grief, and Blake would be damned if he'd let Ty fall.

"Just give me a chance, Ty. Let me help you find some peace."

Ty bit at his bottom lip, worrying it between his teeth for a moment. Finally, after taking a deep breath through his nose and blowing it out, Ty nodded and said quietly, "Okay."

Hiding his own satisfied smile, Blake released one of Ty's wrists and cupped Ty's chin, looking straight into his eyes. "You have your safe words, yellow and red, correct?" Ty gave a slight nod of his head. "That was a direct question, Ty. Answer it correctly." He tightened his grip on Ty's chin. "And with respect."

"Yes, Sir," Ty responded with a heavy sigh. "My words are yellow to slow down and red to stop, Sir."

Blake released Ty's other wrist and dropped the hand on Ty's chin, looping it around his waist, and said, "Come with me."

They moved through the main living room, Ty's breathing speeding up a little as he leaned a little into Blake, and a slight tremor went through his stocky body. Without a word, Blake opened the door to the master bedroom and ushered Ty in. He released his hold on the man, easing around until he was pressed against Ty's muscular back, his arm snaking around the lean waist to the taut stomach and pulling Ty back harder against him. Leaning closer to Ty's ear and inhaling his rich spicy scent, Blake fought his own tremor that threatened as Ty's unique aroma filled his nostrils.

Since he'd first laid eyes on the intriguing cowboy, Blake had wanted him. He still wasn't sure what it was about Ty that affected him so strongly, but he didn't have time to question it. Instead, Blake concentrated on the way the compact muscular body felt as if it had been forged perfectly to fit against his own, the heat of his body. The strong masculine scent enveloping Blake only heightened the effect. Working to keep his voice even, he said, "Set aside everything outside of this room. At this moment, nothing exists beyond these walls and your only purpose is to please me. Do you understand, Ty?"

"I...." Ty cleared his throat, sounding hesitant. "Yes, Sir. I'll try, Sir."

"That's all I can ask." Blake placed a small kiss on the side of Ty's neck, letting the tip of his tongue ghost against the warm flesh, and ground his growing erection against the firm ass, letting the man feel his approval as Ty's flavor filled his mouth. Reluctantly he released Ty and pushed him toward the large armoire. "Go pick any one thing from the cabinet and bring it back to me," he instructed, his voice low.

"Yes, Sir."

Ty stepped forward, opened the armoire, and stood staring at the contents. After a few moments, Ty picked up a cane. He slid his fingers down its length, bending it and caressing the soft leather wrapped around the handle, before returning it to its place. Next, he selected a signal whip made of soft kangaroo, and Blake watched him closely as Ty grasped the handle and let the rest of the whip dangle at his side. He then carefully rolled it back up and returned it to the armoire.

Then, to Blake's surprise—or maybe not so surprisingly, since Ty hadn't denied being a pain slut—he grabbed a flogger. He ignored the soft moose and buffalo hide floggers and went straight for the thick rubber one. Ty brought it back to Blake, holding it out for him.

It was a very high-intensity toy that, when wielded, had a hell of a punch and extreme sting. Ty's choice said much about what he wanted; this flogger would cause extreme pain.

"You're sure?" Blake asked, taking the flogger. "This has a hell of a bite and can easily break the skin." Only if the wielder wasn't careful, and Blake would be very, very careful. There would be none of Ty's blood spilled tonight.

"Yes, Sir. I'm sure."

"Very well," Blake said, his voice low and confident. He took a couple of steps back, giving Ty room to move. "Strip."

"Yes, Sir," Ty answered and began unbuttoning his shirt. Once it was unbuttoned, he left it hanging from his broad shoulders and slid out of his jeans.

Blake took in the sight of Ty's well-defined chest and stomach as Ty folded his jeans and set them neatly on the floor at his feet. The light-blue coloring of the material contrasted nicely against the dark tanned skin beneath. Blake's eyes roamed appreciatively downward to the dark boxers that hung low on lean, narrow hips above strong, well-formed thighs. Ty's body might not have been like those he'd sought out in the past, but he could appreciate the appeal of thick muscles. A body strong from working hard, not built up exaggeratedly like that of someone obsessed with the gym. The shirt joined the jeans, again neatly folded and set on top. Blake smiled to himself, pleased that Ty hadn't made the same mistake he'd made before when he'd thrown his clothes to the ground haphazardly. It gave him more time to appreciate the man before him, and he did very much appreciate the sight. A sudden sliver of excitement worked its way up Blake's spine.

Ty stood hesitantly or perhaps deliberately with his thumbs looped in the waistband of his boxers. Blake suspected the latter, with the slight smile that pushed up the edge of Ty's lip. Either way, it had an effect on Blake, and his cock twitched before Ty slid the boxers down his legs and stepped out of them. Ty then slowly bent, revealing the smooth, deeply tanned skin of his back as he folded the boxers and added them to the rest of the pile.

Blake bit down on the inside of his cheek to hold back the moan that had worked its way up from his chest. Slowly, Ty stood straight again, head bowed, and waited for Blake's next order.

Stepping close to Ty once again, Blake ran his hand over Ty's hip and ogled admiringly. The thick erection stood out proudly from its nest of light curls. When his gaze once again moved up to Ty's face, he could see the tension in the tightly clenched jaw, the tense bulge in the muscles of his shoulders. Ty's body was taut with anticipation, but he was beginning to think beyond the walls of the room. *Unacceptable.* Blake captured Ty's mouth in a demanding and rough kiss, biting at his lower lip.

Ty stiffened briefly; then his focus returned to Blake, and he felt the man melt against him as the kiss deepened and Ty whimpered in response to Blake's teeth and invading tongue. When Blake was sure they were once again the only two in the room, he released Ty's mouth, leaving him panting, and asked in a husky voice, "Are you ready?" Ty wasn't the only one who had been affected by the kiss, and he licked away the last traces of Ty's flavor from his own lips.

"Yes, Sir," Ty answered breathlessly.

"You can either rest your hands against the wall over there"— Blake pointed toward the wall opposite the armoire—"or bend over the bed. I suggest the bed, since I'm not sure how long your legs will hold you once we begin." He slapped the flogger against his thigh for emphasis.

Ty turned without a word and walked toward the bed. He bent at the waist, resting his hands on the cream coverlet, and widened his stance, shifting a few times until he was comfortable. He took a deep breath before visibly relaxing.

Heart beating a little too rapidly, Blake took a moment to calm himself as images of a past life threatened to haunt him. He had ordered Ty to focus on him and let go of the world beyond the room. Ty deserved no less from him. With one last steadying breath, he pushed the last thoughts of his beautiful boy from his mind and focused on the strong body on display before him.

Blake moved closer to the bed. With his free hand, he traced up Ty's spine and back down, the muscles flexing and pushing up into his touch. "Very nice," he purred. "Your skin is beautiful, a perfect canvas for my marks."

"Thank you, Sir," Ty responded softly.

"My desire is to leave my mark upon you. Your only desire is my pleasure. Focus on me, on my needs. Take it for me." Blake took a step back, brought his arm back, and swung, bringing the tails of the rubber against the skin of Ty's right shoulder.

"Fuck!" Ty gasped, his body pulling away slightly from the contact.

Blake didn't respond. Ty was breathing a little harder, but he didn't move out of position. Blake brought his arm down, laying the tails of the flogger on the opposite shoulder. With the next slap, Ty whimpered softly and shifted from foot to foot, but again he held his position.

"I want to hear your voice." Blake struck him again. "I want you to describe what you feel. Scream if you must, but I want an honest response."

"Yes...." Ty groaned as another stroke was laid against his flesh, this time at the small of his back, before continuing, "Yes, Sir. Stings, but in a good way."

Blake set a steady rhythm of light strokes, bringing his arm down again and again. Beautiful red welts swelled above the smooth skin, a deep flush making Ty's back appear to glow. Ty's responses ranged from whimpers and moans when the flogger struck the skin of his back to deep groans and loud screams when the tails landed against the sensitive skin of Ty's thighs. Through it all, Blake studied the man before him carefully. Ty's erection never faltered, instead seeming to swell briefly with each slap of the leather, and he began leaking a steady stream of pre-cum. A deep ache throbbed in Blake's balls, and he looked down at the tented front of his pants. He hadn't even realized how achingly hard he was until the painful throb shot through his sack. Soon he'd have to do something about it, but for now, he pushed his own arousal to the background and once again focused on Ty.

Ty's breathing had quickened but was even and steady. He writhed under the slap of the flogger but no longer cried out harshly. "Oh, God," he panted, his body swaying as if dancing under the blows. "So good, Sir."

It was stunning, watching Ty let go of his anger and all the harsh realities of the world and give in to the pain, rise above the sting of the flogger and find peace as it consumed him completely. "So beautiful," Blake moaned, keeping his arm steady as he watched Ty start to fly. "So gorgeous when you let go," he whispered soothingly. "Do you know how much pleasure you are bringing me? How hot you are like this... how hot you make me."

"Ah God, please... please, Sir," Ty begged as Blake continued to rain down light blows on his ass and thighs.

"Please what, Ty?" Blake asked, moving the flogger back up Ty's back. His arm was aching, sweat rolling down his spine, and his cock was harder than he could remember it being in a long, long time. "Tell you how hard I am? How much I want you. God! You're so gorgeous like this. Your skin red, I can feel the heat coming off your body. Makes me want to bury myself in your heat," he purred seductively.

"Sir... oh, Jesus...." Ty panted harshly, and his body went tense. "So close... please, please...."

"What do you need, Ty?" He stepped a little closer, letting the man feel his own need, his own heat. "Tell me."

"Touch me," Ty moaned, his arms giving out, and he rested his forehead against the bed. "Please... please," he panted over and over, his body vibrating with need.

Blake dropped the flogger to the ground with a thud and ran his hands over his marks, Ty's skin so hot it was like a fire against his palms. He wrapped his right hand around Ty's shaft, pumping the thick cock from base to tip with long, sure strokes. With his left, he continued to explore the heated flesh of Ty's back. "So hot," he murmured. "Does it feel good, Ty? Do you feel the deep ache of my pleasure? So beautiful when you give in to pain, Ty."

"Yes... oh God, yes! So good to me, Sir." His body went tight, hips pushing into Blake's fist as he sped up his strokes. "Ah, fuck... Sir... Sir, I have to come... please, Sir." Ty pulled in harsh pants of breath as he sobbed and begged.

"You very much please me," Blake praised. "Come for me, Ty. Let me hear you, feel you."

Ty gave a relieved whimper that morphed into a deep groan as he started to come. "Ah, God," he moaned as heat splashed over Blake's hand. Blake massaged the abused flesh of Ty's back with his other hand as Ty shuddered through each contraction of his release. When Ty melted, boneless, into the mattress, Blake released Ty's softening shaft, jerked down his pants, and wrapped a fist around his own rigid erection as his other hand continued to knead the muscles of Ty's back. One, two hard pulls and Blake's back arched. "Christ!" he groaned and shot his release over Ty's reddened back and ass.

On shaking legs, Blake grabbed a cloth from the bedside table and cleaned them both up before encouraging Ty under the covers, rolling him onto his side. Then Blake joined him. Pulling the covers up around them both, he spooned against Ty's back, the heat warm and comfortable against Blake's chest.

Sated, Blake closed his eyes and had started to drift off when he heard a nearly inaudible whisper.

"Thank you."

Blake pulled Ty closer and gave in to sleep with a smile on his face.

CHAPTER
ELEVEN

HIS wrists bound to the wall above him, Ty bent his head. His eyes roamed down his own body, a strange tingling feeling tickled the back of his neck, and his stomach tightened as the light from the low overhead bulb reflected off the metal shackles and chains around his feet and spread over his long, slender erection and lean but tight abdomen. His eyes traveled up the length of one long, lean arm to where a shackle surrounded his wrist. He turned his gaze to the man standing before him.

Blake stood in tight leather pants, his well-defined chest rising and falling with his heaving breath. In his hand, he held a heavy-looking leather flogger. He had a devilish smile and a wild glint in his eye as he continued to slap the flogger against his thigh, the sound loud and ominous in the otherwise silent room.

Moving closer until Ty could feel the heat radiating off the man, Blake leaned in, inhaling deeply. "You smell so good." He took another deep breath. "Like sweat, and sex, and all mine." Blake let the tip of the flogger handle ghost along Ty's chest, making him shudder. "Who do you belong to, boy? Who owns all this beauty?"

Closing his eyes, Ty let his head fall back against the brick wall, moaning as a wet tongue and warm lips moved across his neck. "You do, Sir. God, that feels good. All yours."

Ty rocked his hips against the large bulge pressing against him through Blake's leather pants, his chains jangling with his movements. Blake pulled back slightly, a hand wrapping around Ty's cock and a deep growl rumbling up from Blake's chest as Ty's erection twitched against his palm. "Impressive, and all mine. Every inch of this luscious body is mine. Mine to beat, to fuck, to love, always. Isn't it, boy?"

"Yes, Sir," Ty groaned, pushing harder into Blake's fist.

Ty whimpered as Blake continued to stroke his cock and nuzzle the side of his neck. His balls began to draw up as his orgasm tingled at the base of his spine. Without warning, Blake growled again and bit down hard on the thick tendon at Ty's neck. Ty yelped at the unexpected pain, and his eyes flew open. An agonizing howl rushed out of him as his eyes met his reflection in the mirror on the wall across the room. Only they weren't his pale-blue eyes staring back at him; they were deep, chocolate brown. Lorcan stood staring back at Ty, the mirror reflecting him with Blake wrapped around him, Blake whispering against Lorcan's neck what a perfect boy he was, how much he loved him and that he was never letting him go.

Ty bolted upright in bed, and he panted harshly, trying to catch his breath. "What the fuck," he muttered, scrubbing a hand across his face. "Stupid fucking dreams."

"Go back to sleep, it's too early," a voice said next to him, causing Ty to jerk his head toward the sound. The sun was just coming up, and he easily recognized Blake's dark head against the white pillow, his eyes closed as he reached out toward Ty. Before Ty could pull away, Blake made contact with his chest and pushed him back on the bed. Ty hissed when his back made contact with the mattress, causing it to sting.

"Sorry," Blake muttered and wrapped himself tightly around Ty, holding on.

It took Ty a minute to become aware of where he was, the dream still riding him hard, making his stomach roll, and his heart pounding painfully in his chest. It didn't take a rocket scientist to figure out what the dream meant. Lorcan had weaseled his way into Ty's dreams to remind him how much better he was than Ty.

The night before had been so amazing. Blake had kept his promise, taken him out of his head and sent him flying. It had been the first time in what felt like ages since he'd found a little peace, and wasn't it fitting that Lorcan had destroyed it by weaseling into his dream. The first time he found happiness, Lorcan destroyed it. His first moment of peace, Lorcan destroyed it. Hate as black and thick as sludge seeped into Ty's system, filling every cell of his being, nearly choking him with the rancid flavor it left in his throat.

Lorcan, with his perfect tall, lean body, perfect chestnut hair, perfect olive skin, perfect sunny fucking disposition, wouldn't stop at just taking Quinn. No, he wouldn't stop until he pushed Ty to the breaking point, taking everything from him that brought him the slightest sliver of peace or happiness. *Not if you get rid of him. Lorcan is nothing. No one. Don't let him take what belongs to you, your happiness.* Ty squeezed his eyes shut, his body tensing as the black hate infused the thoughts in his head. The ugly part of him, the part that was tired of being pushed around, left alone and feeling insignificant, screamed at him to stop sitting around and fight!

Suddenly a crushing weight was on top of him, and Ty struggled to free himself. His head thrashed from side to side, his back bowing up off the mattress in an attempt to throw off the man now pinning his hands above his head, his thighs restrained by muscular, unforgiving legs.

"Ty, that's enough," Blake demanded. "Stop! It was just a dream."

"Fuck you! Get off me," he bellowed, his voice sounding more like that of a wounded animal than his own.

Blake pressed down impossibly harder against Ty and, ignoring his rants, took Ty's mouth in a punishing kiss. It really couldn't be described as a kiss, more like a clash of tongues and teeth that left them both panting with broken and bleeding lips when it ended.

"Right here," Blake said, pulling back and staring down at Ty with intense black eyes. "Focus right here on me. You had a bad dream, it wasn't real." Then Blake was kissing him again, this time tenderly, teasing his lips, softly asking for entry.

Ty made a small sound like a whimper as he opened his mouth, tasting blood, and felt the gentle slide of Blake's tongue against his own. Exhausted, he stopped struggling, relaxed back against the mattress, and focused on Blake's strength still holding him tightly and the taste of blood, tears, and desire as Blake continued to explore his mouth.

This time when the kiss ended, Blake rested his forehead against Ty's and asked, "Better?"

Ty gave a slight nod, still feeling a little off balance from the sudden shift in emotions, but yeah, much better.

"Do you have to go to work this morning?"

Ty stiffened as he remembered the last thing he'd said to Quinn the day before. He'd told the cowboy to enjoy his fucking life and screamed, *"I quit,"* as he hopped into his truck and peeled out of the drive. No way in hell could he work on Quinn's ranch and watch the preparations for their upcoming wedding without going completely postal. *Christ, now I have no job, no Quinn, and I still want to fucking kill Lorcan. If the pansy boy wasn't in the picture, my—*

A stinging bite to Ty's bottom lip stopped his dark musings. "Stop it!" Blake demanded again. "It was a simple question, Ty. Do you have to work this morning—yes or no?"

Ty ran his tongue over his dry lips, easing the sting and tasting blood. Bastard had cracked open his lip again. "No! Now you want to get off me?"

"Good. Here is what you are going to do," Blake said calmly, ignoring Ty's demand. "You're going to get up and take a shower. While you are in the shower, you're going to think about what you will be cooking us for breakfast. If you're not done showering once you've figured out breakfast, you're going to then come up with what to do after breakfast to please me."

Ty laughed, an ugly sound, not one with a single trace of amusement. "You have got to be fucking kidding me."

The hands around Ty's wrists tightened, and Blake tightened the muscles in his lower limbs, spreading Ty's legs, pulling and stretching the muscles of Ty's thighs until Ty gasped as a burning pain shot both up and down his body. "Ty," Blake said in a low voice, yet the effect was like a hard slap. "Get in the shower."

Blake stared down at him with a patient look on his face, yet his dark eyes were fierce. *Oh, for fuck's sake.* "Fine, you pushy bastard, get off me."

Blake didn't move, just continued to stare at him expectantly. Ty's consciousness narrowed to the muscles of his legs and arms as the sensation of aching burn moved into screaming pain. In that long stretch of agonizing silence while Blake continued to stare at him, Blake became his focus, and he found himself answering, "Yes, Sir."

"Good man," Blake praised and released Ty's limbs before rolling away and leaving the bed. "I'll set out a towel and toothbrush for you on the bathroom counter," Blake said as he moved into the master bathroom. "There is also deodorant, razors, or anything else you might need in the cabinet below the sink. Help yourself."

Massaging his wrists, Ty sat up and watched Blake move into the bathroom. He swung his legs over the side of the bed, wincing as the muscles throbbed, and noticed his reflection in the mirror on the dresser. It was his own reflection looking back at him, his shoulder-length blond hair disheveled and standing on end, his own familiar blue eyes and scruffy face. He was still staring at himself when Blake returned from the bathroom, grabbing a pair of sweats from the dresser and pulling them on.

"I'll give you a hint, Ty. I like my eggs over easy," Blake tossed over his shoulder, and he left the room.

Surprisingly, Ty stood and headed to the bathroom to take a shower, thinking about eggs, bacon, and a variety of other breakfast foods.

OTHER than to ask where to find a pot, a spatula, or whatever else he needed, Ty didn't speak while he prepared breakfast, and Blake sat at the kitchen island, sipping coffee and watching him work. Ty looked more comfortable in his own skin than Blake had ever seen him, and when Ty was at ease, he was even more handsome than Blake had first thought. His blond hair was darker in appearance while damp, and his smooth shaven chin and broad back looked sexy as hell, Blake thought with a sly smile, with his marks still red and glowing.

Another thing that heightened Ty's good looks was the way he hummed quietly as he worked with confidence while he flipped eggs, turned bacon, and toasted bread. Ty was sexy when he was angry too, but Blake had an animalistic, aggressive response to it. He wanted to command and control all that strength rather than appreciate Ty's appearance. But this new Ty, the Ty that had a calm aura surrounding him, was definitely tripping every one of Blake's arousal triggers. Blake's desire was evident by the way his shaft was pressing hard and throbbing against the soft material of his sweatpants and by the sweet tingling along his nerve endings.

Ty set a plate carefully in front of him with a shy smile on his face and set another plate on the empty spot across from Blake before returning to the counter, grabbing the coffeepot, and bringing it back to the island. "Would you like more coffee, Sir?"

Blake doubted Ty even realized he had just called him sir, and he was outrageously happy that his initial gut feeling about Ty was correct. The man was a natural submissive. When he was given a task to do, he didn't think, he just did it. Blake smiled and set his mug down. "Yes, please, and breakfast looks and smells wonderful. Thank you, Ty."

Ty's smile grew, and he preened at the compliment as he poured coffee first into Blake's cup and then into the cup he'd set out for himself. After returning the pot to the coffeemaker, Ty took the seat across from him. Blake hesitated, then bit the inside of his cheek to keep from showing his delight when Ty sat but didn't pick up his fork until Blake did.

Blake picked up his fork and took a bite of the hash browns Ty had fried with onions, peppers, and spices. "This is great," he murmured at the delicious flavor.

"Thank you." Ty grinned and took a bite of his own.

"So tell me," Blake inquired, taking another bite before continuing. "Did this lovely breakfast take up all your thoughts in the shower, or did you have time to mull over other things?"

Ty laughed softly. "I had a few extra minutes to mull a few things over." He snorted and grinned, then said, "Though I'm not so sure I followed your second order all that well."

Blake picked up his mug and raised it to Ty. "Do tell," he encouraged before taking a sip.

"Well," Ty said slyly, "I'm not sure what your particular tastes are when it comes to pleasure, so I may have stuck in a few of my own fantasies instead of thinking of how to please you."

Blake's cock twitched, and he had to take another sip of his coffee to ease his suddenly dry throat before responding. "Oh, I don't know, Ty. I'm pretty versatile and enjoy a wide range of pleasures. I have a feeling you and I may have one or two that are the same." Blake winked at Ty. "In addition to bondage and being naked, since we've already established those similarities."

Ty met his eyes for the first time since they'd entered the kitchen, and he studied Blake playfully. "I never admitted to liking bondage or being naked."

Blake raised an eyebrow and set his mug down. "You didn't have to, and I'm sure you're not going to deny what your body was screaming at me."

Ty didn't say anything immediately. Instead, he smiled while dabbing his toast into his egg and taking a bite, swallowing before he answered. "Nah, I'm not going to deny it. Kind of hard to after the scene last night." Ty shrugged and finished his toast and started in on his bacon.

Oh, he loved when his gut steered him right, and looking at the flushed skin of Ty's face and the sly smile on his lips, he was going to love even more hearing what Ty had been thinking about while he finished his shower and shaved. "Well, let's hear what kind of pleasures you were thinking about."

Ty finished the slice of bacon he'd been chewing. "It didn't take very long to figure out what I could make for breakfast. I'm not all that great in the kitchen, but I can make a mean breakfast."

"That you can," Blake agreed, finishing the last of his hash browns.

"Thanks." Ty waved off the compliment. "So anyway, once I figured out what I could cook, I started thinking about Qu—nothing in particular, and I started getting a little...." Ty huffed out a heavy breath, his shoulders slumping as he struggled to get his thoughts in order.

"It's okay, Ty," Blake encouraged in a low, even voice. Ty's irritation at Quinn was seeping back into his eyes and the way he held his body, and Blake redirected the man's thoughts quickly before the seed of anger could grow. "Just start where you started thinking about the pleasurable things. Was I using a crop or a flogger? Were you in full bondage or just your wrists?"

Ty shook his head, took one more deep breath, and visibly relaxed. "I started out thinking about bending over and offering you my, um, assets." Ty snorted. "And then I thought about going down on you. But... well, I know those things would bring you pleasure, but as my imagination got a little more intense, it just kind of took on a life of its own, and the next thing I knew I was thinking about being tied to a St. Andrew's cross, full deprivation, and...." Ty shrugged. "It kind of morphed into all the things that brought me pleasure. Sorry."

Each new thing he learned about Ty only served to intrigue Blake further. He barely knew Ty, but what he did know of the wonderfully complex man in front of him he found very fascinating and yearned to know much, much more. In some aspects of Ty's personality, he reminded Blake of a child with ADD, moving from one thing to another smoothly, almost effortlessly forgetting about what he'd just been thinking of, as he had when shifting from his anger at Quinn to thinking of what to cook for breakfast and how to please Blake. Yet he could also focus single-mindedly for long periods, as he had proven with breakfast and the flogging the night before. A handsome, complex, and high-spirited submissive was an unusual find, and Blake would have to remember to thank whoever it was that looked over deviants and had sent him out to catch Ty spying on two lovers that day. The fact that Ty had admitted that full deprivation was one of his pleasures was also a testament to how complicated Ty Callahan was. He was a puzzle that Blake had every intention of solving.

"Those must have been some interesting imaginings, considering you made breakfast looking as if you were floating on a cloud," Blake teased. "What tools do you like?"

Ty bit at his lip as he considered thoughtfully what Blake had asked. "I don't know if I can pinpoint one thing I like more than another. I mean, I get off on crops and floggers, but a bullwhip in the hand of someone who isn't sure with their strokes sucks. On the other hand, in the hands of a skilled Dom, it's one of my favorites. I guess that's true of most toys. All of them can be a favorite or hated implement, depending on who's wielding it." Ty looked up from his empty plate and met Blake's eye. "What about you? What gets you off?"

"What doesn't get me off would be a better question." Blake chuckled and pushed his own empty plate away.

Ty reached out to take Blake's empty plate, then hesitated briefly, catching himself before asking, "Would you like more?"

"No, thank you, Ty, I'm finished," Blake responded, watching intently while Ty picked up their plates and took them to the dishwasher, returning with the coffeepot and refilling both their cups before taking his seat once again.

Ty clasped his hands around his mug, staring searchingly at it as if he would find the answers to the question evidently troubling him in the dark liquid.

"Ty, I don't have any secrets, and you can't offend me, so just ask whatever it is that is troubling you."

"Does humiliation and torture turn you on?" Ty asked uncomfortably without looking up. It was apparent from the way Ty held himself and spoke the words that he found both disturbing.

"No!" Blake said adamantly. "I shouldn't have been so flippant in my response. I apologize. What I should have said is that I can use most toys, and use them well. I prefer floggers and crops. I also like all forms of bondage, but what really gets me off, what I really take pleasure from, is watching someone submit." Blake reached a hand across the table and lifted Ty's chin until the man was looking at him before he continued. "I'm an aggressive and strict Dom, but I'm never cruel, okay?"

Ty relaxed visibly and nodded.

Blake let go of Ty's chin and stood. "C'mon, I want to show you something."

CHAPTER

TWELVE

THE room Blake led him to had high ceilings with exposed log rafters. The floors were a beautiful rustic barn wood polished to a shine, yet the room was completely empty. The walls were stark white; the single small window was devoid of curtains or any other type of covering. The only color in the room was the dark green of the sweatpants around the lightly tanned body of Blake Henderson as he stood in the center of the room, his arms outstretched.

"So what do you think of my playroom?" Blake asked Ty pointedly.

"A little barren, wouldn't you say?" Ty responded, standing only a few feet from Blake and giving him a questioning look.

"Yeah, well...." Blake dropped his arms to his side and looked thoughtfully around the room before stepping up closer to Ty and meeting his eyes. "I get off on dominating a man, controlling his reactions, but it's about mutual pleasure. I never abuse or mistreat anyone, but they will ache." A dark look passed briefly across Blake's eyes, but he covered it up quickly. "You asked me about torture and humiliation. This empty room is a direct result of when those things go too far. I will not ever engage in either one."

Ty returned Blake's gaze, studying the man. For the first time, Ty really looked into those dark eyes looking back at him. What he saw he recognized immediately. Ty had seen it enough in his own eyes when looking in a mirror—anger, betrayal, and heartbreak—but he couldn't understand why Blake would have a similar look. Blake, who knew who his parents were, had a nice home, money, and all the things Ty lacked. But how could that be?

"I don't understand," Ty finally admitted with confusion.

"I want you to stay here," Blake responded.

Now even more confused, Ty asked, "Excuse me?"

"I think you and I can help each other. I can help you let go of your anger, and you can help me rebuild my playroom."

Irritation at Blake began to prickle Ty's skin. He didn't need to let go of his anger, he just needed to use it productively, like coming up with a plan to get rid of Lorcan. Blake had helped him rein in his anger, and he felt like he was now better in control of it, instead of it controlling him. Ty wasn't unappreciative, but now he had some planning to do. "You know what?" he muttered easily. "My anger and I don't need any help, and I suck at construction and remodeling, so I'm just going to go." Ty started to walk away in search of the rest of his clothes when Blake's hand on his arm stopped him.

"You can't stop Quinn from marrying Lorcan any more than I can bring Eli back."

Ty shrugged off Blake's hand and glared at the meddling son of a bitch. "I don't know who Eli is, and I'm sure he had his reasons for leaving, but it has nothing to do with me or my anger."

"You're right," Blake said bitterly, returning the glare. "Your anger has nothing to do with Eli, but I've seen what jealousy can do. It will eventually destroy you, and anger that stems from that jealousy can destroy the lives of others. Give me one week, Ty. Seven days of your submission, and if at the end of the week you still feel the need to send another message, then have at it."

Ty's eyes widened, and his heartbeat sped. *Fuck! He knows.* Stunned, he searched Blake's eyes. *He has to be guessing, listening to speculation and unsubstantiated rumors. I've been careful. He can't know.* However, Blake's face was unreadable. The bastard either had one hell of a poker face, or he knew. Ty's eyes narrowed. "Are you threatening me?" he accused.

"No," Blake responded softly. "I'm offering you an outlet for all that anger simmering just below the surface. I admit, I don't know the whole story, but if I know you're behind the messages, then I guarantee you others have their suspicions as well. Give me one week. I guarantee you I can help you control your anger. What do you have to lose, Ty? If you still want to go after Quinn at the end of the week, then at least you'll go about it thinking more clearly. What do you say?"

Denying it seemed ridiculous. "What's in it for you?" he asked with suspicion. "What do you get out of it?"

"I get a new playroom." Blake winked, trying to lighten the mood, but the small smile he gave Ty didn't reach his eyes. The sadness Ty had seen earlier was still there, though now it was infused with a light of determination.

"What are the terms?" Ty asked noncommittally.

The smile on Blake's face grew. "I'll take a quick shower and we'll discuss the terms. Deal?"

What the hell. If he didn't like what Blake had to say, he could still walk away. He'd just have to be more careful with his plans in the future. And if he did, well... Blake was right, what did he have to lose? Ty shoved his hands in the pockets of his jeans. "All right, I'll listen to what you have to offer."

"Great!" Blake responded, satisfied. He pecked Ty on the cheek as he passed him, heading toward the door. "I'll be quick. Go ahead and finish getting dressed, and I'll meet you in the living room." Blake stopped just outside the door and turned back to face Ty. "And Ty?"

"Yeah?"

"A new playroom isn't the only thing I'll get." He turned and strolled down the hall.

Ty had no idea what Blake was talking about, but by the mischievous look on Blake's face before he had turned away, Ty could just imagine.

COMFORTABLY lounging on one of the oversized recliners, Ty scanned over the list of Blake's likes and dislikes. The document was a glimpse into Blake's anal personality. Not anal as in physically, though Ty hoped he was, but anal in the sense that the list was so complete and organized it read like a business flowchart. Flipping the sheet over in his hands, Ty covered his mouth and snickered. Had he really expected pie charts and a graph?

"What's so funny?" Blake inquired from where he lounged next to Ty in his own oversized chair.

"I was just wondering where the flowcharts were?" Ty ducked just in time to dodge a pillow whizzing by his head.

"Just read it and stop being so damn cheeky." Blake lowered his voice and grumbled, "What am I getting myself into?"

Ty bit down on his lip, but a small snort escaped. He hid behind the paper in his hand from the glare Blake shot his way.

Ty enjoyed teasing the man, but he was also acutely aware of the excitement swirling around in his gut and his arousal heating his blood, pooling in his groin. He'd never actually signed a contract with a Dom, but he'd read plenty of contracts between subs and Doms at the club. He'd also spent plenty of time feeling envious of those who had found someone they could trust enough to enter into such a commitment with. Seven days wasn't a true contract, but for Ty it felt like a huge deal. The light feeling seeped from him and perspiration dampened his brow, and he wiped it away with the back of his hand as the pleasant feeling of just moments before turned to nausea. What the hell was he thinking? He shouldn't even be considering something like this.

"Stop thinking too deeply, Ty," Blake said evenly, interrupting Ty's internal panic. "This isn't a long-term commitment or a difficult negotiation. Just read the paper in your hands and tell me what you think."

Ty peeked up over the top of his paper, ready to snap off a snarky comeback, but Blake was looking at him thoughtfully with a patient look, and the words died in Ty's throat. It was irritating how Blake seemed to be able to read his thoughts after knowing him for such a short period of time, but it also piqued his interest. *Freaky, but interesting.*

Turning his attention back to the paper in his hand, Ty read over Blake's list. None of the things on Blake's favorite list surprised him. Floggers, crops, bullwhips, and canes were among his favorite implements. Also not surprising was Blake's fancy for bondage, role-playing, and administering discipline. Ty rolled his eyes that Blake had added orgasm to his list of favorites. Well duh, who didn't like orgasms? He and Blake also had a few dislikes that were similar, and he was glad to see humiliation, permanent scarring, and water sports added to Blake's dislike list. But seeing all forms of edge play on the dislike list was unexpected.

"What have you got against edge play?" Ty asked, setting the list on the table between their chairs. "I'm going to be honest, I totally get off on being pushed to the edge," he admitted.

"That type of play takes a lot of trust. If I were in a long-term committed relationship with my sub, then those things would be on my favorites list." Blake shrugged without apology. "Anyone who plays on the edge with someone they barely know isn't just dangerous, they're stupid."

It could be dangerous and stupid with someone you trusted as well. He'd experienced some of the most intense orgasms during edge play with Brian, especially with oxygen deprivation. He'd been young, reckless, and willing to do anything to please his Dom back then and had nearly paid the ultimate price for his misplaced trust. Ty nodded. "I can understand that."

"Any other questions about the list?" Blake asked.

"Nope." Ty waved a hand in Blake's direction. "Let's hear what your terms for the week are, and I'll let you know if I can accept them or not."

Blake picked up his glass from the table, looking at Ty, appearing to consider his words carefully. He took a sip from his water and set the glass back on the table before speaking. "It's simple. I want your complete submission. That's not to say the week will be simple or that it won't be hard. I meant it, Ty, when I told you I am a very demanding and strict Dom. You will be obedient, respectful, and give up complete control to me for the next week. Your only purpose, while you're here, your only thought, will be me and my pleasure."

What Blake was offering sounded like a dream vacation. To be able to set aside the shit that had become his life lately sounded like heaven. But, like the old saying went, if it sounded too good to be true, it probably was. Submitting was no problem for a single scene, for a couple of hours, but a week? He wasn't so sure he could do that.

Who are you kidding? You can barely get through an hour. Ty pushed himself up out of the chair. "I'll give it some... I'm going to go." He ran a frustrated hand through his hair, rubbing at the throb that had started at the back of his skull. "I'm going to head home. Give me a couple of days and I'll let you know."

Blake rose smoothly to his feet and in two long strides was standing within Ty's personal space. "You don't need a couple of days to think about it, Ty. You need to stop thinking altogether and just be." Blake ran a soothing hand down Ty's arm, and he found himself pushing into the touch. "You need this, Ty." The comforting hand moved around to Ty's back, massaging and pulling Ty closer to the man's heat. "It's now or never."

Then all thoughts of lists, submitting, anger, and everything else fled Ty when Blake's warm, demanding mouth covered his. The kiss was fierce, and Ty found himself falling into it, and he was given another glimpse of the peace the dominating man was offering him. And fuck, how he wanted what was being offered. Ty was left dazed when the kiss ended, his forehead resting against Blake's as they both fought to catch their breath.

"One week, Ty. Nothing heavy, and you have your safe words. All you have to do is focus on me and my needs and be honest in your reactions."

Ty clung to Blake, his hands fisting in the man's T-shirt, holding on as he searched Blake's eyes. Ty wanted this. For whatever reason, he believed the man could deliver, maybe at some level even trusted the confident cowboy could give Ty exactly what he needed. He found himself melting into Blake's heat, letting go of his misgivings, and he nodded in agreement. "All right, I'll try."

"The only thing you can't safe word is to leave before the end of the week. You can stop anything else, but I want your word that you'll stay until the end."

Ty pulled back slightly so Blake could see how serious he was. "You have my word. I'll just run home, grab some clothes, and be back this afternoon. We can begin then."

"You won't need clothes, and I'll provide everything you need this week."

"I can't walk around here naked all week," Ty squeaked. He might get off on exhibitionism, but in the club or under certain conditions, and stomping around a ranch in front of a bunch of ranch hands was not his idea of ideal conditions.

Blake held tighter to Ty, refusing to let him pull away. "Trust me to give you what you need. I'm not going to humiliate you, remember? This week will be just you and me. No one else, okay?"

Taking a deep breath and letting his body relax further against Blake's strength, Ty lowered his eyes. If he was going to do this, he might as well give it his best. Who knew, maybe Blake was right and the Dom could help him. *I hope so,* he thought sincerely. With one last deep breath, Ty slid to his knees at Blake's feet. "Yes, Sir."

An audible sigh of relief came from above Ty, and Blake's fingers threaded through Ty's hair gently. "Thank you."

They stayed where they were, the silence in the room stretching out, but not uncomfortably, as they each took a moment to let what was about to happen sink in. Ty focused on the soothing hand in his hair, let go of his apprehension, and waited to see what the Dom would do next.

Startled, Ty blinked up at Blake when instead of giving him a command, he tipped Ty's head back, bent at the waist, and pressed a soft kiss to Ty's mouth. "Let's give you a tour of the rest of the house. After lunch, we'll go over everything I expect from you this week in greater detail. You'll have the opportunity to ask any questions you want while we eat."

"Yes, Sir." Ty stood, keeping his eyes low.

Blake walked to the kitchen area, Ty following close behind. Pointing to a door at the end of the counter, Blake said, "If you can't find something, check in there first. You'll be responsible for all our meals. I'm not picky, but I do like variety in my meals."

"Lucky for you, I am, if not the best cook, then at least imaginative," Ty teased, following Blake out of the kitchen.

"No, that would be luck in your favor. Saves you from having to learn quickly and no doubt a few strokes," Blake countered easily.

Ty followed Blake through the rest of the house, appreciating the beauty of the large log home. He'd gotten a glimpse of Blake's office but was told it was strictly off limits. He was also shown the storage room and where the cleaning supplies as well as the clean linens were kept. Most of the spare rooms were barren like Blake's playroom, and he didn't have to concern himself with those. In the master bedroom, Blake pointed to the bathroom. "I'm a neat freak, so I expect you to keep this room tidy and clean up after yourself." Blake gave Ty a wink. "I'll give you a little hint how to please me: I love long, hot baths, even more so when I have someone to wash my back." Blake strolled to the large king-size bed and sat on the edge, patting the space next to him.

Ty dutifully followed the gesture and sat next to him. "This is the only other room you have to worry about until we start working on the playroom. I have someone who comes in three times a week to clean, but think of this room and the master bath as our space. You'll keep it clean at all times and make sure it's fully stocked with condoms and lube." Blake waved a hand toward the armoire. "You'll find extra supplies in the bottom drawer if the bedside table drawer runs low. I also suggest stocking them in the bathroom, kitchen, and living room." Blake arched a brow, his look devilish. "It's your ass, after all."

"I'll keep that in mind." Ty laughed, the last small traces of apprehension gone with Blake's responding chuckle.

Blake's hand landed on Ty's thigh, a jolt of arousal shooting up from the contact, an arousal that increased when he looked up and met the man's smiling face. "Let's go have lunch, and I'll give you a rundown of the rules. The sooner we get that out of the way, the sooner we can start concentrating fully on my pleasure."

Returning the smile, Ty stood. "I live to concentrate on your pleasure, Sir." A hard slap to his ass made Ty yelp.

Blake stood and brushed past Ty, causing a shudder to run through him when Blake grumbled, "I'm going to take much pleasure in spanking that smart ass."

CHAPTER
THIRTEEN

LUNCH had been a delicious chicken Caesar salad, and Blake had been impressed with how Ty worked so efficiently and with ease when given a specific task to focus on. He'd given Ty a rundown of a few basic rules and been beyond pleased that Ty had been attentive and had felt comfortable enough to ask questions when appropriate. He'd also been relieved, since it showed that, at least for the moment, Ty was taking their arrangement seriously.

Not wanting to overwhelm Ty with too many rules all at once had only been part of his motive for rushing through lunch. Blake felt like a kid on Christmas morning and couldn't wait to get his hands on his gift. And Ty's submission was a gift. Sitting on the edge of his bed, he took in the sight of Ty standing before him; Blake ran the leather of the single-snap cock ring through his fingers, anticipation hardening his shaft further.

"Strip, then come here and stand in front of me." His voice was even, not betraying his eagerness.

"Yes, Sir."

Ty removed his clothing quickly, leaving it in a neat pile at his feet before moving to where he'd been directed. Unlike before, Ty stood with good posture—his shoulders straight, hands clasped behind his back in a proper display position. He had been at ease since starting lunch, and without his anger clouding his mind, Ty slipped easily into a submissive role.

Blake reached out and wrapped his hand around Ty's semi-soft shaft, pulling a small moan from the man as he stroked his cock in long, firm strokes until it hardened in his fist. Only then did he snap the cock ring into place, Ty's moan turning into a groan.

"Poor man," he said with mock sympathy, continuing to pump Ty's cock. "Be thankful I thought of it. Now you will be able to focus more on me."

"Aren't you just thoughtful, Sir," Ty replied with a hint of sarcasm in his voice.

"Shall I take it off, then?" he deadpanned, the fingers of his free hand hovering near the snap. He might be enjoying himself a bit too much, but what fun was having a sub if he couldn't enjoy it?

"No! I mean… the cock ring was very thoughtful, Sir. Thank you, Sir," Ty said with real thankfulness, his voice having lost the cockiness at the threat.

"Smart man," he praised, releasing Ty's shaft. Blake smiled at the relief-filled sigh that escaped Ty. If Ty knew what was coming next, Blake doubted he'd be relieved, but why spoil his surprise? Without teasing the man any further, Blake grabbed a tube of lube from the bedside table, palming it and pulling himself to his feet. "Stand in the center of the room, bend at the waist, back straight, and grab the backs of your knees. We're going to try this again."

Ty nodded and moved into position. Blake didn't correct him for not replying. He hadn't asked a direct question, and as easy as they were with each other at the moment, he knew it wouldn't last. Once he started to push Ty to his limits, he was sure he'd be seeing Ty's anger flare again. This time, when Blake stood before Ty and reached out to caress his hair, Ty didn't flinch. Instead, he pushed into Blake's touch. A small pleased smile curled Blake's lip at the gesture, especially when Ty's shoulders relaxed even further as the caress continued.

"I'm going to inspect you now," he warned Ty. "Remember, I want only honest reactions from you. You're not to come and you are to warn me if you get close, understand?"

Ty shifted slightly, widening his stance before answering, "Yes, Sir."

The pose would make Ty feel vulnerable, but that wasn't the reason Blake had made him assume this particular pose. It gave Ty the opportunity to look down without having to worry about seeing or being distracted by Blake's roaming hands. Blake also wanted Ty to get used to the feel of his hands on him, wanted him to be accustomed to it. If he was not completely at ease, then maybe he would at least start to trust that Blake had no intentions of abusing him.

Blake started at Ty's feet, running his hands up and down the well-defined muscles of Ty's calves, moving up his muscular thighs. The man was in wonderful shape, and Blake had a new appreciation of a thick, muscular body. Blake didn't linger on the taut globes of Ty's ass; he'd explore that part of his anatomy soon enough. Instead, he moved up to Ty's back, outlining the small white scars that marred the tanned skin. A couple of the scars were much larger than the others, the tissue built up excessively, indicating that they had once been severe injuries. He was curious to know if they were a result of the lifestyle or simply from an accident. Blake made a mental note to ask Ty about them later, not wanting to inadvertently remind Ty of painful memories right now. After examining Ty's head and the entire circumference of his neck, as well as exploring the thick muscles of Ty's chest and finding the man in what appeared to be top physical shape, he finally moved to stand behind Ty.

After opening the lube and pouring a generous amount onto the fingers of one hand, Blake reached between Ty's spread thighs and cupped his balls gently, feeling their heavy weight before moving up to stroke Ty's thick erection. He ran his fingers down the soft skin, feeling it throb at his touch. "I've never been fond of bulky muscles, but you have given me a new appreciation. You're in wonderful shape, and your body pleases me very much," he purred.

"Thank you—" Ty's breath caught as Blake eased the tip of one slick finger back to press against Ty's opening. "Thank you, Sir." Ty released his breath with a moan as Blake slipped the tip of one finger inside. "Ah, God. That feels good, Sir. I'm glad you're impressed."

Blake hadn't meant to do anything more than inspect Ty for scar tissue or any other signs of damage, but with the way Ty clenched around Blake's finger, he found himself fighting to keep control. "Very much," he said absently.

Ty gasped and shifted his position from one foot to the other as Blake moved his finger in and out slowly, pushing deeper. "Hard... so hard, Sir."

"Close?" he asked.

"Not yet, Sir," Ty panted. "But you keep doing that and I will be."

"That's the point," Blake cooed, speeding up the thrusts of his finger. Ty was breathing heavier, but his body didn't seem overly tense.

Ty was stunning when he gave in to pleasure, the flex and roll of his muscles as he gently swayed to the rhythm of Blake's thrusts. His skin flushed deep with arousal, and his soft moans of "oh, God" and whimpers of bliss filled the room. Blake stood transfixed at the sight of the magnificent man in front of him, his own cock twitching wildly and his balls heavy, as Ty's tight passage opened up to him. Blake gently slid a second finger alongside the first. This was how Ty should always sound, moaning with ecstasy rather than snarling with anger.

"Sir! Fuck... close, Sir," Ty cried out, pulling away from Blake's hand, his body bowstring tight as he took in great gasps of air.

Blake froze as Ty struggled to control himself, and then withdrew his fingers, placing his other hand on the small of Ty's back and rubbing softly. "And I was so enjoying myself." Blake pouted playfully.

Ty shook his head. "Obviously I was too, Sir," Ty chuckled. "Christ, that was close."

Perhaps a little too close, but Ty had followed his order, and that was what mattered. Blake crossed back to the armoire, tossing the lube into a drawer. He wiped his hands on a towel and pocketed a condom. "You seemed to be focusing a little too much on yourself. Now it's my turn to be the object of all that focus. On your knees."

"Yes, Sir." Ty groaned as he stood, briefly stretching his back and legs before going easily to his knees. He kept his hands clasped behind his back and his eyes lowered.

Blake stood inches from Ty and threaded his fingers through Ty's long blond hair, massaging his scalp. "Only fair I get close, don't you think?" Blake asked, pulling Ty close.

"I think that's very fair," Ty murmured, nuzzling Blake's cock through the denim of his jeans.

"Show me."

Ty mouthed Blake's erection through the denim, his warm breath heating Blake's flesh. Blake continued to massage Ty's head, grinding his crotch against Ty's hungry mouth. "Do you still want to fuck me, Ty?"

"No. Not really, Sir," Ty muttered against Blake's crotch, sounding embarrassed.

Blake hadn't thought Ty got off on topping, but he didn't want to make assumptions either, so he'd given Ty the chance, in case he'd been wrong. Blake nodded to himself, satisfied with Ty's response. "Do you enjoy anal sex?"

"Fuck yeah," Ty said enthusiastically, looking up at Blake. "I'm a total bottom for a reason." Ty seemed to catch himself, his cheeks turning red, and he lowered his eyes. Ty went back to nuzzling Blake's crotch and murmured, "Sorry, Sir."

Blake chuckled. "It's okay, Ty, I'm glad you enjoy it. I don't have to use sex to get my sub's attention or to give him what he needs. I can use a wide variety of tactics to get his submission without the sexual aspect. Bondage, inflicting pain if it has a purpose and is meaningful, I very much enjoy, but when someone submits to me sexually as well, all the better." Blake ruffled Ty's hair, then caressed his cheek. "Your response, while not quite respectful, pleased me very much."

Ty pushed further into Blake's touch, a small sound issuing from the man with the simple praise. Ty was starved not only for affection but for approval as well. Blake could use his need to get what Blake needed, what they both needed.

"Take me out, Ty," he said, continuing to stroke Ty's cheek. "Suck me," he whispered.

Ty reached up for Blake's jeans, popping the button and lowering the zipper slowly. With a gentle hand, he slipped his fingers into Blake's boxers and released his straining shaft. In infinitely gentle strokes, Ty ran his fingers over the silky skin of Blake's cock, humming his approval as it jerked at his touch. With his free hand, Ty pulled Blake's jeans lower, fully exposing Blake's cock and balls before leaning in and running a tongue around the head and then lower to lap gently at his balls.

A low growl rumbled in Blake's chest. The gentle ministrations of the man before him were in sharp contrast to Ty's powerful body, heightening Blake's arousal. He stared down his body, entranced, as Ty gently pulled one ball into his mouth, licking gently, Ty's wicked tongue running along the silky skin before releasing it and drawing the other into his mouth. Blake couldn't wait to be buried balls deep in that blistering wet heat. Grasping the base of his aching cock, Blake threaded his fingers in Ty's hair with the other hand, tugging back until Ty let Blake's sac slip from his mouth. "Open your mouth."

"Yes, Sir," Ty responded immediately and opened his mouth wide as instructed.

Blake held Ty's head and pushed the tip of his cock past Ty's parted lips. Ty wrapped his lips around the head and began to suck. Pulling back on Ty's hair, Blake withdrew his cock, holding it inches from Ty's lips. "I said only open your mouth." When Ty complied, Blake once again pushed his cock past Ty's lips. This time Ty held his mouth open wide, keeping perfectly still, and allowed Blake to push deep. "That's it," Blake praised, sliding in and out of Ty's mouth.

After a few thrusts, Ty completely relaxed and allowed Blake to set the pace, and he fucked Ty's mouth in long slow thrusts. Pulling back until the tip of his cock was at Ty's lips, Blake released his hold on the man's hair and ordered, "Suck!"

Ty complied immediately, wrapping his lips around Blake's shaft and sucking hard. Ty's cheeks hollowed as his head began to bob, and he surrounded Blake's cock in perfect wet heat.

"That's it, Ty. Focus on my pleasure. Let everything else but me, my pleasure, go."

A moan of approval reverberated up the length of his cock as Ty sucked. Ty's lips stretched around the base of his cock and his tongue slid along the sensitive underside. The intensity with which Ty sucked him stole Blake's voice, but he lifted one hand to Ty's head and petted him, encouraging him with his hand instead of his voice. Ty took the gesture for what it was, opening wider. The pace at which he took Blake in and out of his mouth increased. The wet sounds of Ty's moans and mewls as he hummed against Blake's throbbing cock proved his desire to please Blake.

Ty continued to suck eagerly, pulling Blake deep into his throat, driving Blake to the edge of orgasm when he swallowed, throat constricting around Blake's cock, only to pull back and suck gently again. Curling his hands around Ty's head, Blake took control. The orgasm that began to tingle at the base of his spine wouldn't be held back much longer. With a low growl, he held Ty's head still and began thrusting deep and hard into the perfect wet heat of Ty's throat.

Ty gave up control completely, becoming pliant in Blake's hands and allowing Blake to set the pace. On the verge of detonation, Blake faltered as his balls cinched up high and tight. His legs wobbled, and Ty reached up, placing his hands on Blake's thighs, steadying him while digging his fingers in.

"Close," Blake warned. "God, yes! So good, Ty."

Heat surged through Blake, and he forced Ty off his shaft. Keeping one hand fisted in Ty's hair, he grabbed his cock with the other and pumped his release with a loud shout over Ty's face and neck. When he was finally empty, Blake released the death grip he had on Ty's hair, steadied himself by placing a hand on Ty's shoulders, and leaned on the man's strength as he fought to get his breathing under control. Once he could speak again, he looked down as Ty wiped away Blake's release from his eyes, cheeks, and nose. "Christ, you're good at that," Blake chuckled, his breath still not as steady as he'd like it to be.

"Thank you, Sir," Ty said with a wink. "I take pride in my abilities."

"As you should," Blake responded honestly as he pulled his jeans back up, leaving them undone. He walked to the cabinet and snatched up a towel, bringing it back to Ty and handing it to him.

"Thank you, Sir," he said again and took the towel, wiping it down his face and neck, a satisfied smile on his face. When he was done, he set the towel aside and lowered his head, waiting for his next order.

Blake looked down on him and took in the flushed skin and dark ruddy cock standing proudly from his body. Ty's cock looked painfully hard, but he held himself as if he were completely at ease, his breathing slow and even and his hands open and resting on his thighs.

"Come here, Ty," he said softly.

Ty looked up, a confused expression on his face, but he did as Blake instructed, rolling to his feet with grace and taking the few steps toward Blake until he was standing in front of him. The confused look changed quickly to stunned when Blake wrapped his hand around Ty's neck and pulled him into a kiss. Ty opened up to the kiss, swaying slightly as Blake explored his mouth. Their tongues slid along each other, and they both moaned softly. Blake deepened the kiss, teasing and tasting, leaving them both breathless when it ended.

"I think that deserves a long, hot, relaxing bath. Wouldn't you agree?" Blake asked, placing one last kiss on Ty's swollen lips.

Ty looked down his body briefly and tried to hold back his pitiful groan but was unable to hide it completely. "Yes, Sir," Ty responded through gritted teeth. "I think that's a wonderful idea."

"I thought you would like that idea." Blake laughed, grabbing a pouting Ty's hand and leading him to the bathroom.

CHAPTER
FOURTEEN

WASHING Blake's back while the man lounged in a hot bath hadn't been Ty's first choice of what was a *good idea*. After watching Blake come, tasting him on his lips, Ty could think of a lot better ideas than soaking in a tub. First on the list was ripping off the cock ring and shooting his load. Now, as he lay back against Blake's chest, the warm water surrounding them, he had to admit that it was, in fact, a fabulous idea. He loved the way he felt wrapped in Blake's arms as his hand caressed soothingly up and down Ty's chest and stomach. He'd expected to be angry over being denied his release, even lash out at how unfair it was that Blake was sated while he had been left unfulfilled. But strangely enough, he didn't feel unsatisfied at all. He was even beginning to like the way his hard shaft throbbed lightly in the same slow rhythm as his heartbeat.

"What are you thinking about?" Blake whispered against his ear.

"I was just thinking that I should be pissed off that you got a nut and I didn't, but I'm not," he admitted.

"Aches so good, doesn't it, Ty?" Blake asked, running his hand down Ty's body to gently cup Ty's erection. "Looks good too."

Ty looked down his body, his cock a deep red, jutting up obscenely with the black leather of the cock ring wrapped around the base. His prick throbbed and twitched as Blake continued to tease at it with his fingers, the side of his hand teasing his balls. Yeah, it did look good. The steady throb was no longer irritating but familiar, and he welcomed it. He couldn't remember ever being so hard yet so completely at ease. It was a strange feeling, but in some weird way it felt right. He reached down, grasped his straining shaft, and squeezed lightly.

"You're touching yourself. Tell me what you're doing. Be specific." Blake nipped at his ear, a shudder running down Ty's spine at the sting.

"I ache. It helps ease it," he lied. He tightened his grip, biting back the moan as a painful jolt shot to his balls.

"No touching yourself without my permission," Blake ordered, swatting his hand away.

"That's impossible. If you haven't noticed, it's attached to me. Besides, it's mine."

"Not this week it's not." Blake grabbed Ty's wrist, pulling his hand away before he could grab his erection again. "This week it belongs to me, and I'll tell you when you can touch and when you can't."

This wasn't only an impossible order to follow, it was also ridiculous. "I have to wash, use the bathroom. You know, all the necessary things. Scratch."

Blake chuckled and nipped his ear again. "Let me rephrase that. No touching yourself sexually without permission."

Ty tried to pull free from Blake's grasp, a thrill running down his spine when Blake not only held fast but grabbed his other wrist as well. "Define sexually," he said, a hint of defiance in his voice. Like he'd be able to control himself in his sleep, and it wouldn't be completely his fault if he happened to shake it a couple extra times, and if he just happened to come, well… that wouldn't count.

"Any touch that's meant to arouse is sexual. And don't even think about trying to blame it on sleep. I'll be cuffing your hands at night, so you won't have to worry about *accidentally* touching yourself."

"You're not serious!" he said incredulously.

"Oh, I am quite serious, Ty. I could always put you in a cock cage at night if you prefer?"

"No!" Ty shuddered. He hated those fucking things… sort of. "And what happens if I break the rules?" Not that he was agreeing to this new rule, but he was still curious.

"If you follow the rules, you get rewarded. If you break them, you'll get punished."

Ty tried to pull away again, but Blake held fast. He tried another tactic and pressed his ass hard against Blake's cock, rolling his hips. "Yeah, tell me about your rewards and punishments," he purred seductively, continuing to roll his hips.

Blake hissed, his cock hardening against Ty's ass. Blake crossed Ty's arms over his chest and pulled them tight, stopping his movements. "I can see punishment in your very near future. Rewards will be coming, being fucked, sucking me off…." Blake traced the shell of Ty's ear with his tongue, pulling a moan from him before continuing, "Spankings. Punishment will be not being allowed to come after I fuck you, leaving you aching in a cock cage while sucking me off, tying you up and forcing you to listen to my CD collection of Don Knotts singing the best of Broadway."

"Oh, God! Anything but Don Knotts. No, Master! No." Ty laughed.

"Then we have an understanding." Blake laughed in return. He released Ty and pushed him forward, encouraging him to sit between Blake's spread thighs, and began washing his back. "Let's get you washed up, then. Tonight we'll order takeout, lounge on the couch with a movie, and head to bed early. Tomorrow, I want to put you in deep submission, and you're going to need your rest."

Ty moaned as Blake scrubbed his back, and he melted as the Dominant massaged shampoo into Ty's hair. The sweet ache in his cock and the thought of snuggling on the couch next to Blake consumed his thoughts, and he nodded his agreement.

THE early-morning rays of dawn lit up Blake's room just enough that he could study the figure lying next to him. Blake hadn't bound Ty's hands the night before as he had threatened, choosing instead to let his hands remain free so Blake could feel them caressing him as he held Ty in his arms, Ty's head resting on his chest. Ty now reclined next to him, his hands together as if he were praying, resting below the pillow underneath his head. He knew Ty was much younger than his own thirty years, but when Blake looked at him now, completely at ease in slumber, he looked not only young but also so innocent. The wary look in Ty's eyes and the numerous marks along the skin of his back told the tale of a harsh life, but lying here vulnerable in sleep, Ty brought out all of Blake's protective instincts. And wasn't that just ironic as hell.

Looking down on the sleeping cowboy with his regal nose, strong chin, and silky blond hair, he could see why he'd been so drawn and aroused by Ty Callahan. However, the good looks hadn't been what had driven Blake to seek out Ty. Nor were they what had driven Blake to invite the man to live in his house for a week. It had been Ty's anger that had called to him so strongly, and that was where the irony came in. He had wanted to protect Quinn and Lorcan from Ty's anger, to prevent what happened to his Eli from happening to anyone else, and yet here he lay, feeling protective of the very man he wanted to protect others from. Blake's heart twisted painfully in his chest as he thought of what anger and jealousy could do, what they could destroy.

A small sound escaped Ty, and pale-blue eyes blinked sleepily up at him, pulling Blake away from his painful thoughts before they could form completely and crush him. "Good morning," Ty murmured, stretching leisurely.

"Good morning. How'd you sleep?"

Ty moved, stretching his arms, legs, and back as if he were making a rundown of his body's condition before answering. "Obviously like a log, without experiencing any hot and horny dreams. My dick hurts," Ty complained with a pout.

Blake threw his head back and laughed. It wasn't that he didn't have any sympathy for Ty's condition, but he was ridiculously happy that Ty's focus was on his dick rather than on his anger and thoughts of revenge on Lorcan and Quinn. "You poor, poor man," Blake purred, kissing the pout on Ty's lips. "If you're very good today, perhaps I'll see what I can do about taking care of that little problem."

Ty lifted the sheet covering him and looked down his body. "Little problem?" he asked, arching a brow.

"Okay, fine." Blake snorted. "Your massive, huge, gigantic, awe-inspiring problem."

"Damn straight." Ty winked, satisfied. He glanced back down his body where his erection tented the sheet, curling toward his belly. "Okay, so maybe not so straight," he amended with a shrug. "So what's on the agenda for the day?"

"No pun intended, I'm sure." Blake groaned at Ty's bad joke.

Blake had learned quickly that Ty responded better with one task to focus on. The man was also a sensualist and hedonistic. Now that he was growing accustomed to the ache in his cock, the sensation of a warm bottom would make it less likely that his mind would wander. Blake threw off the covers and sat on the edge of the bed. "First things first. C'mere, Ty," he instructed, patting his lap.

Ty eyed him suspiciously but threw off the covers and stood at the end of the bed, a couple of feet from Blake, who was opening and closing his hands over and over. Ty looked down at Blake's lap and complained, "You're kidding me, right?"

Ty's words may have suggested he didn't want what was coming, but his cock jerked, a small pearl of precum appearing at the slit. Ty's body betrayed him; he wanted what Blake was offering very badly.

"I'm completely serious, Ty. Bend over my lap, hands resting on the floor and ass up in the air."

Ty stood still, blinking at him. Blake could see Ty struggling with what he wanted and what he thought was the right thing to do. Blake took the decision out of his hands when Ty continued to hesitate. Ty was thinking too hard. "C'mere, Ty, not because you want to, but because I need you to. Focus only on my pleasure, my needs."

Blowing out a big breath of air, Ty walked the last two feet on shaky legs and stood closer. Blake tugged Ty down, the man falling into his lap, his hands reflexively going to the floor to support his weight. "Good job," Blake praised, running a soothing hand over the taut skin of Ty's ass. "Give me your submission, Ty. I want it. You need it," Blake said with confidence.

Ty took another shuddering breath and blew it out, visibly relaxing against Blake before saying, "Yes, Sir," in a quiet voice.

"Remember, this is about my pleasure. You have your words. Use them if you need them."

"Yes, Sir," Ty responded, shifting his feet until he was comfortable and pushed his ass out. Ty blew out one last breath before responding. "Your pleasure. I'll remember, Sir."

Blake started with light slaps to Ty's ass, just enough to give Ty sensation but no real pain. The pain would come from the sheer number of repetitive strikes. He had no desire to hurt Ty, only to help him stay focused. He wanted Ty's attention to stay on him, on what they would be doing together over the course of the day. As Ty began to push into the slaps, Blake increased the force of the blows, the sound of each swat loud in the otherwise silent room.

"Ah, stings," Ty moaned after a few of the more forceful blows.

"I know," Blake said softly as he continued to pepper Ty's ass. "Take it for me, Ty. Take it because it pleases me."

"Yes, Sir," Ty moaned, panting lightly with each stinging blow.

Ty's ass began to glow a nice rosy blush, the man grunting and swaying with each blow. Blake slowed his hand, lightening each slap, bringing Ty down slowly, finally stopping and resting his hand against the warm flesh, enjoying the heat against his palm. Blake praised Ty. "Very good. Red looks good on you," he teased lightly, helping Ty up and pulling himself to his feet.

He placed a soft kiss to Ty's panting lips. The man looked blissed-out and accepted the kiss with a lazy smile on his handsome face. "Thank you, Sir. Red feels good too."

"You're welcome." Blake smiled, pleased with himself for having read Ty so well. The man would be amazing to watch in the kitchen, and if Ty's thoughts strayed from fixing breakfast, Blake knew exactly where they would wander. He pinched the abused flesh of Ty's ass, making him yelp. "Now, I'm thinking pancakes would be perfect for breakfast." His stomach growled its approval.

CHAPTER
FIFTEEN

BLAKE moved around the kitchen, making coffee and generally just keeping an eye on Ty. The man worked efficiently, and if left alone to prepare breakfast on his own, he would be fine, but where was the fun in that? Besides, Blake found himself drawn to the happily humming man while he worked. As Ty flipped the pancakes on the griddle, Blake reached out and grabbed a handful of reddened ass, squeezing the tight muscle through the soft fabric of Ty's sweatpants.

"Ow," Ty yelped, followed by a chuckle as he twisted out of Blake's reach and pointed his spatula at him. "Don't make me spank you."

"Oh no, I think that's you who gets spanked," Blake said, waggling his brows at Ty and stalking toward him.

Laughing, Ty slipped out of his reach once again. Blake looked over at the griddle filled with light-brown pancakes, a delicious scent wafting up from them. He pointed to the griddle. "I think they're burning," he said, a plan forming in his head.

"What?" Ty squeaked, rushing to the griddle and right within Blake's reach.

While he was otherwise distracted with flipping his cakes, Blake took the opportunity to press against Ty, grabbing his hips and pressing his growing arousal up against Ty's ass. Ty's attempt to wiggle out of his grasp didn't have the desired effect, and instead Blake ground harder against the sweet ass.

"Would you go sit down and let me finish these? I'm going to be pissed if you cause me to burn my breakfast." Ty's words were grumbly, but the way he pushed against Blake betrayed his real desire.

"Fine," Blake conceded, placing a kiss to the side of Ty's neck before releasing him. "What do you need me to do to help?"

"Sit and stay out of my way," Ty responded lightly.

"Brat," Blake grumbled and took a seat at the island. "How much longer?"

"Two minutes. Now quit bugging me." Ty went back to his task, uttering a barely audible complaint under his breath. "Pushy Dom."

A grin spread across Blake's face. It was going to be pure pleasure showing Ty just how pushy he could be, but for now he'd behave.

Ty grabbed a couple of plates from the cabinet and plated the pancakes. He looked good, moving around the kitchen with ease. He went and fished around in the fridge, coming back with fresh berries and whipped cream. Adding the fruit and cream to the pancakes, Ty brought the plates to the island, setting one in front of Blake, the other in the empty space across from him.

"Do you want coffee?"

"Sure, coffee sounds good," Blake responded with a smile. Ty turned, a shy smile on his face, and went to grab the coffeepot. While Ty's back was turned, Blake grabbed Ty's plate and pulled it across the island, next to his own.

"I prefer a more... up close and personal breakfast," Blake responded to Ty's suspicious glare when he brought the coffeepot to the island.

"More personal?" Ty questioned, filling both mugs.

Fuck! Ty's shy smile was sexy, sending Blake's blood rushing to his groin. "Yes. More personal. It's about my pleasure, is it not?" Blake patted his lap. "I can't think of anything more pleasurable than being fed by you." It would also nicely distract Ty from thinking until he could get the man into deep submission.

Ty shrugged, setting the pot on the island, then sat gingerly on Blake's lap. A sweet pink blush colored Ty's cheeks even as the man pushed down against Blake's thigh. "You know, this would be easier if you let me sit in my own chair."

"It's not about easy," Blake murmured, placing a hand on Ty's thigh and curling his fingers around it. "It's about being close and enjoying your body while you feed me."

Ty grabbed a fork, speared some pancake, fruit, and cream, and brought it to Blake's mouth. "Open up."

Blake opened his mouth, accepting the bite, moaning his approval at the sweet flavor. He could feel Ty's eyes heavy on his mouth as he licked at the corners of his lips, and he couldn't help but teasing a little, running his tongue slowly around his lips.

"Is it good?"

"Mmm... very good, but I think I need another bite to be sure."

"Don't be so greedy," Ty teased with a smile. He took a bite for himself before offering another to Blake.

"I bet you earn a lot of spankings," Blake commented around another bite. "You're very naughty, aren't you, Ty?"

"The threat of spankings isn't much of a deterrent for being naughty," Ty said with a chuckle, offering Blake another bite.

Ty stopped him from responding by shoving another bite into Blake's mouth. Enjoying the food, Blake made little sounds of approval and moaned softly with each bite. Ty kept alternating bites between them. The heat of Ty's reddened ass against his thigh and the little porn noises Ty made around his own bites were heady. The sexual arousal sparking and swirling around them was thick in the air, wrapping around Blake, heating his skin and hardening his cock.

Ty, the little minx, wasn't helping Blake hold on to his quickly shredding control. Ty wiggled his ass, pushing hard against Blake's cock as he took the last bite of pancake and fruit. Groaning, Blake pushed Ty off his lap. "Christ, I'm not super human," he complained through gritted teeth.

Ty chuckled, moving quickly around the island, avoiding Blake's swat, and took the seat across from him. Blake spread his legs a little wider, giving extra room to his painful shaft, and glared at a smiling

Ty. "You know, your teasing isn't going to make me want to go easy on your ass later," Blake warned.

Ty grabbed his coffee cup, took a sip, and looked up over the rim with heavy-lidded eyes. "Who said I wanted you to take it easy?"

Blake's cock throbbed.

Before Blake could respond, the first explosive sign of Ty's anger, still smoldering just below the surface, appeared when a ringing from the bedroom interrupted the calm, easy feeling of just moments before.

Ty set his mug down stiffly and wrapped his hands around it, holding on tightly as if it might fly away if he let go. He didn't comment on what was obviously his cell phone.

"Aren't you going to answer that?" Blake asked, pushing his empty plate to the side.

Ty tensed further and shook his head before bringing the mug to his lips and taking a sip of his coffee.

"What if it's important?"

"It's not," Ty grumbled around his mug.

"Whoever it is, it's obviously upsetting you. Want to talk about it?"

"I fucking said it's no one!" Ty roared, standing and shoving back so quickly the chair tipped over, crashing to the floor. He ignored it, dropping his coffee cup in the sink with a thud as he stomped by.

"Ty, come back here," Blake ordered, coming to his feet.

Ty responded by storming into the master bedroom and slamming the door. Only one person Blake knew of could make Ty react like that. Ty must know it was Quinn calling him. Either him or Lorcan, but he had a sneaking suspicion that it was the former. Picking up the toppled chair, Blake pushed it back into position close to the island and took his mug to the sink. After one last sip of the calming brew, he poured the rest in the sink and set the empty cup on the cupboard. Blake flicked off the coffeepot as he walked by. Neither of them would need any more caffeine today.

Blake turned the knob without knocking and entered the master bedroom. Ty had already pulled his T-shirt over his head and was slipping into his jeans when he entered. As he lifted his foot to slide on his other pants leg, Blake took advantage of Ty being off center and grabbed him from behind, wrapping his arms around Ty's chest and arms.

"Fucking turn me loose, Blake. I'm not in the mood for any games." Ty struggled against him, but Blake held on, pulling a snarling Ty toward the bed.

As soon as the backs of Blake's legs hit the bed, he forced them down to the floor, leaned back against the bed, and laid his legs over Ty's thighs, effectively pinning him. "You're going to stop being disrespectful and take a deep breath." Blake added a growl to his voice, which caused Ty to still for a moment.

Ty, being the more muscular of them, could easily throw Blake off if he wanted to, but he didn't. The submissive in him responded to the authority in Blake's voice, and Ty took deep breaths as he'd been instructed. Blake held him close, letting Ty feel his strength and draw his own from it. They stayed there, wrapped in each other, for a long time, the heat of Ty's body solid and warm against Blake's chest. Blake didn't speak or try to rush the man, just held him for as long as he needed it. Slowly, Ty's breathing evened out, and he lowered his head and relaxed fully. Other than a sigh, Ty remained silent.

"I'm not going to order you to tell me why you're so upset," Blake said softly. "But I would like you to tell me. Keeping all that anger inside isn't healthy, Ty."

A strangled sound escaped Ty, and he began to tremble slightly in Blake's arms. Blake didn't push, but silently he prayed Ty would trust him enough, at least in this. When Ty's breathing once again returned to normal, the trembling in his muscles beginning to ease, and still he hadn't said anything, Blake decided to try another approach to get the man to talk. The subject didn't matter; he just needed Ty's focus on something other than the anger. Sure Ty would run if pushed too hard, he picked a safe topic. "I was watching you sleep this morning, and you looked so young and innocent, and it struck me that I didn't even know how old you are."

"Twenty-two," Ty responded, his voice sounding raw.

"Wow, I was in my teens when I came out to my family and close friends but was your age before I felt comfortable enough admitting it to anyone else. You seem so comfortable with who you are. I'm going to assume you were younger?"

"I always knew I was different than the other kids. When some of the other foster kids were sneaking looks in the girls' room, hoping to get a peek of them undressing, I was looking at the boys. I think I was about eight or nine when I was moved to another home and one of the older boys told me he was gay. I didn't really understand the word. I mean I had heard it on the playground, but just like fag, I thought it was something bad because kids always used it when they were being mean." Ty shrugged. "Anyway, this older kid, I don't remember his name, but he explained what it meant and I was like, hey, that's me. I'm gay. It was also that day that I learned to keep that shit to myself or you get your ass kicked on the playground."

Ty spoke easily, the topic simple, familiar, and safe, as he continued to relive the past, the anger of only moments before forgotten. Ty completely relaxed against Blake, snuggling in closer, the fingers of one hand drawing designs on Blake's arm. "I wasn't embarrassed for being gay and never denied it, but I didn't go around broadcasting it either, ya know. Then, when I got put out at eighteen, I met Brian, and after that I said fuck it. If anyone had a problem with the fact that I was gay, it was his or her problem, and I guess I still feel that way. Life's too short to pretend I'm something I'm not."

Blake doubted that Ty realized how much he had revealed about himself, and thought he would probably be embarrassed if he knew. But the way Ty talked so casually about being moved to another house and said he'd "got put out" instead of "moved out" when he turned eighteen spoke of a kid with a history of being shuffled through the foster system. Blake was curious at what age Ty had entered the system, and about his parents, but he finally had a relaxed man in his arms, and he wasn't ready to upset that just yet. It was another thing he added to his mental list to come back to later.

"How old were you when you realized you were submissive?" Blake asked, keeping his voice conversational.

"I don't think I had a great epiphany one day and started kneeling at men's feet and letting them smack my ass." Ty chuckled. "Brian was heavy into BDSM and a Dom, so I naturally fell into the submissive role."

"Was Brian your first Dom?" Blake asked curiously.

"My one and only, more than a single scene Dom, if you can call him a Dom. I think of him as a sadistic prick who preys on vulnerable men."

"That's quite a harsh term."

"Yeah, well, it's fitting." Ty started to pull away, and this time Blake let him go. Jumping to his feet, Ty kicked off the jeans that were pooled around one of his legs and started to pace. "I don't want to talk about Brian."

"Okay," Blake said, pushing up and sitting on the edge of the bed. "What do you want to talk about? You're obviously still agitated, and I want to help you let it go."

Ty ran a frustrated hand through his hair. "I don't want to talk about anything. I don't...." Ty blew out a frustration-laced breath before stopping and staring at Blake with pleading blue eyes. "I don't want to talk, I don't want to think, and I just want to be still and...." Ty's shoulders slumped. "I just want to feel what I did this morning."

"You want peace," Blake said quietly. Standing, he crossed the room and stood in front of Ty. He reached up and ran a soothing hand down Ty's arm. "Yeah, we can find you some peace, but I want to revisit these topics later. I won't push, at least not right now. But I think it's important for you to talk about them and deal with them so you can finally let go of the bitterness you feel, okay?"

"Yeah, okay," Ty replied, and he nodded. He then lowered his eyes and pushed into Blake's touch. "Yeah... yeah, later is good," he whispered. Then, to Blake's shock, Ty fell to his knees and pushed his cheek against Blake's thigh. "I'm sorry, Sir. I'm sorry I disrespected you." His breath hitched as he spoke, true regret evident in his voice.

Jesus, just a small amount of kindness, a simple touch, and Ty broke. Was this why Ty was so obsessed with Quinn? Had the ranch owner shown Ty a little bit of the kindness that Ty so desperately craved? Blake reached down and cupped Ty's chin, encouraging the man to look up. The panicked and lost look in Ty's eyes stole Blake's breath. As he held Ty's gaze, staring into those sad, scared pools of blue, a crack began to form in the carefully constructed wall Blake had erected around his heart.

As much as the idea of punishing Ty for his offenses bothered him, not to punish the man would be doing a great injustice to Ty. The moment Ty fell to his knees and offered Blake his submission, his apology, Blake had a responsibility to either accept what Ty offered or to walk away. Since Blake did not intend to walk away, he had to allow Ty to redeem himself.

Blake stroked Ty's cheek with his thumb. "Mistakes happen, Ty. What's important is that you take responsibility for your mistakes, make amends, and learn from them. Punishment is about learning from mistakes and being forgiven. You've earned three strokes."

"Yes, Sir," Ty responded with a relieved sigh, some of the panic in his eyes diminishing. "Thank you, Sir."

"You're welcome." Blake helped Ty to his feet, wrapping him in his arms. He hid his own shaking hands by fisting them in Ty's T-shirt and pulling the man harder against him.

CHAPTER
SIXTEEN

AFTER spending the rest of the morning with a subdued and quiet Ty installing a swing in the playroom, Blake ran a critical eye over the device. As Ty knelt naked in the display position in the center of the room, Blake ran his hands over each leather strap and double-checked each buckle and joint for flaws. There was now a large blemish on what he'd hoped would be a peaceful day of heavy submission for Ty, but he wasn't going to dwell on it. Ty had apologized for his outburst and disrespect and had accepted his punishment. Blake meant to salvage what was left of their day and give Ty some of the much-needed peace the man craved. Tomorrow he would push.

"Come here, Ty," Blake ordered, keeping his voice low.

"Yes, Sir." Ty quickly rolled to his feet, keeping his head down, and moved up close to Blake.

Blake studied the man before him. He'd never been one to demand a submissive keep his eyes lowered. In fact, he'd told Ty that he didn't have to keep his eyes lowered unless he ordered him to do so. He enjoyed looking into his submissive's eyes. Eyes were the one feature on a person that rarely lied. Blake had always thought of eyes as little windows, smudged with color and fancy curtains to hide behind. If you could look past the fake emotions hung as window treatments, the true person would be revealed. Ty, though, felt safe keeping them lowered and only rarely gave Blake real glimpses of him. Eventually Blake hoped Ty would trust him enough to always meet his eyes.

Without the benefit of Ty's eyes, Blake instead took in the way Ty's chest rose and fell evenly as he breathed. From his good posture, without extra tension tightening his muscles, and the quiet calm surrounding Ty, he knew the man was in a good headspace. Blake touched Ty's arm gently so as not to startle him when he spoke in the silent room. "I know you like full sensory deprivation, but I'm not comfortable with that level of bondage with a sub I don't know well enough or with a sub whose trust I haven't completely earned. However, your body will be tightly bound and in my complete control. You'll be blindfolded. You'll have your ears and your voice, and I expect you to give me honest reactions. Understood?"

Ty studied the blindfold and light flogger as well as the soft terrycloth towel and tube of lube Blake had laid out on the floor within easy reach. Ty then rolled his shoulders and opened and closed his hands a couple of times before saying, "Yes, Sir, I understand."

Blake moved Ty until he was in the right position. "Sit back on the swing, holding on to the suspension straps, and I'll help you to lie back."

Ty took a strap in each hand as instructed, tensing slightly when the swing began to sway as he sat down.

"I've got you," Blake murmured soothingly. Steadying the swing, he encouraged Ty to release his hold on the straps and, with his hands supporting Ty's shoulders, helped him to lie back until the swing was supporting his full weight. Blake then secured Ty's legs and arms, carefully checking each strap to make sure none were twisted or tied too tightly. Ty followed his movements with his eyes as Blake checked each inch of the swing again.

"How does that feel?"

"Feels good, Sir."

"The leather isn't pinching anywhere? Any spot you feel you need more support?" Blake inquired. If he was going to help Ty get into the right headspace and let go, he didn't need anything to distract from it.

Ty moved his arms and legs as much as the restraints would allow, open and closed his hands again, even wiggled his toes. He took a deep breath and expanded his chest as far as it would go, then lifted and lowered his head. "Perhaps a little more support for my neck."

Blake grabbed the soft towel from the floor, folding it to make a small pillow to add more support for Ty's neck. Once it was in place, Ty lifted and lowered his head again, closed his eyes, and took in a couple of deep breaths. "It feels good, Sir."

Trusting that Ty would tell him if he needed anything else and that he was in fact comfortable, Blake grabbed the blindfold from the floor and secured it around Ty's head. "Can you see anything?"

"No, Sir."

Blake took in the sight of Ty bound and blindfolded. The dark color of the leather straps stood out in sharp contrast to Ty's smooth skin. The black leather strap wrapped around the base of Ty's hard cock caused a flush of heat to surge through Blake. A thrill raced down his spine as it hit him that this magnificent and strong man was completely at his mercy, that he was the master of all those powerful muscles. Blake reached out and ran a fingertip from Ty's throat to his breastbone, then swirled it around each peaked nipple. Ty moaned softly as Blake continued to explore the skin of his chest.

"You should see yourself, Ty. So sexy bound in all this leather." Ty's breath caught when Blake ghosted a finger along the hard ringed cock. "Your beautiful cock straining, twitching and begging for my touch," he praised, lowering his voice until it was a soothing tone. "Clear your mind of everything but me. When you don't hear my voice or feel my touch, listen for the sounds of my movements, my breath."

Blake bent and grabbed the lube, slipping it into the back pocket of his jeans. He had left it out, along with the blindfold and flogger, to give Ty a hint of what was to come. Next, he picked up the flogger and moved back close to Ty.

"Relax. Your only job is to relax and focus on me. Your body is mine. Mine to touch, to position, to play with. Your mind is mine. All you have to do is be." Blake used his voice to lull, to soothe. "Please me, Ty. Give me your mind and your body because it pleases me." He ran the tails of the flogger down Ty's side, up across his chest. "Mine to strike, because it pleases me." He let the soft tails skim along Ty's engorged shaft, watching it twitch. "Mine to stroke and to fuck, because it pleases me," Blake whispered.

Ty took in a breath sharply as the tails of the flogger tickled against the silky skin of his cock, but made no other sound. Other than the throbbing movement of his shaft, he kept his body still, freely giving himself over to Blake's will.

Blake nodded. Confident that Ty was comfortable and finding a calm headspace, Blake moved around Ty without speaking. He randomly touched the inside thigh of one leg, his chest, his arms with the flogger. "There is only me, Ty. No anger, no betrayal, nothing beyond this room that can touch you. Think about what you want to be, what you can be, when you give yourself to me." Gently, Blake pushed the swing with his free hand and started it swaying slowly.

He watched the gentle rise and fall of Ty's chest, the occasional involuntary twitch of muscle. Ty's lips were parted as he breathed evenly, his face slack without any outward appearance of stress. He was beautiful. Blake moved to stand near Ty's bound legs and gently brushed the flogger against the backs of Ty's thighs and ass. Slowly but steadily, he began to swing the flogger, putting a little more strength behind it. A low sound rumbled up from deep in Ty's chest as the contact of the flogger increased. It was a content, peaceful sound, like the whisper of a light breeze or a pleasant, distant melody. Blake continued a slow buildup, adding more power until the resounding slap of leather against Ty's skin added to the harmony of Ty's song. He moved in a repetitive pattern, down Ty's left leg, across his ass, up his right leg, and then following the same pattern in reverse. Ty's pleasurable sounds grew louder, becoming guttural as they peaked, and then complete stillness and silence. Ty was flying. Blake continued his pattern, slowly lessening his strokes until they were whispers of touches, before stopping altogether.

TY'S skin tingled; there was no longer any real pain as the flogger made its rounds, just warmth, heating his skin. As the strokes continued, Ty's focus narrowed. He could feel each individual tail of the flogger as they caressed his skin briefly before sliding away. Then nothing. It was as if he had entered a state of suspended animation. Time, place, even his physical body ceased to exist, and he floated. There was no sound, not the whisper of his breath nor the beat of his heart, just complete and utter silence. There were no smells, no sights, nothing but a swirling of strange muted colors dancing around him.

How long Ty floated, he didn't know, nor did he care. For the first time in his life, he understood what true peace was. Not just peace like what could be achieved with a quiet, warm bath or a deep dreamless sleep, but a peace Ty felt in the pit of his soul. He floated and just was.

A careful measured sound was the first thing Ty became aware of, and he tried to ignore it. A strange pressure pushed at the cloud of color that surrounded him, increasing as it pushed at random intervals. Ty winced, momentarily frightened when a loud roar filled his ears, until he realized it was the sound of his own beating heart and the air moving in and out of his lungs. A tingling. A heaviness to the cloud, and then the slap. Ty gasped when, in a blink, he fell back into his body and he was aware of someone stroking the skin of his thighs, the sensation almost too much to bear, as if all of his nerve endings had come alive at once. Ty could feel the panic beginning to surge through his system, and then he heard Blake's low, familiar voice. "I'm here. Come back to me, Ty." His voice was calm and soothing. The whispered touch of Blake's fingers was replaced by a stronger, deeper touch along the insides of his thighs, sending sparks to dance along his skin.

Ty took in a deep breath, blowing it out as the tingling sensation increased. He swallowed, licking at his dry lips.

"That's it," Blake purred. "Come back to me."

Blake's warm breath tickled the side of Ty's neck as he whispered in his ear. "Close your eyes, Ty. I'm going to take off the blindfold."

He closed his eyes, and the blindfold fell away. Even the filtered light through his closed lids seemed harsh, and he squeezed his eyes tightly against the unwanted stimulus.

"Open your eyes, Ty. Let me see those gorgeous baby blues," Blake urged quietly against his ear.

Slowly, Ty blinked open his eyes, and it was as if the last switch on an electrical panel had been flipped and all of Ty's systems were back online, firing at once. The air rushed out of his lungs in a whoosh, and he gasped at the intensity of the sensations racing through him. "Oh, God," he moaned, the sound raw and gravelly from his dry throat.

Blake's warm lips against his ear set off a chain reaction. The tingling feeling raced down his body, and Ty became keenly aware of the straps tightly hugging his body, the tight band around his painfully throbbing cock, and the heaviness in his balls as they drew up snug against his body. "Oh, God... Sir?" he panted, not even sure what he was saying. He was so fucking turned on, it felt as if he would burst.

Blake nuzzled his neck. "Tell me what you need, Ty."

"You... fuck... Sir! Take me." He was babbling; he knew he was but couldn't help it. He needed to come, now!

The growl that erupted from Blake was a deep animal sound, mingling with Ty's desperate, needy moans and whimpers filling the room. "Christ," Blake groaned, moving quickly to position himself between Ty's spread and bound legs.

"Please, please...." Ty panted harshly and then screamed when a slick finger stabbed into him. Ty's focus narrowed to the thick digit sliding in and out of his ass, the way his passage clamped down on the invading finger, trying to pull it further into his body. Then there was another sliding alongside the first. "Thank you, Sir," Ty grunted. His body trembled, and sweat rolled down from his temple. "Oh, God, Sir...."

Ty whimpered when Blake pulled his fingers free and then sighed in relief when he felt the sheathed head of Blake's cock pushing against his entrance. Ty tried to relax as Blake slowly began to enter him, inch by excruciatingly slow inch, but his body was thrumming with need, clenching and jerking. The burn was hot, and Ty gasped, damn near unable to pull air into his lungs as the burn turned into white-hot heat. Ty's heart stopped beating and his breath stuck in his lungs as Blake continued to push deep. There was just the burn, only the burn.

"Fuck, fuck, fuck," Blake cursed, buried deep in Ty's clenching ass. Blake held still, his body trembling with the force it took. "Ah, fuck, Ty," Blake gasped. "Please tell me I can move."

Ty couldn't speak; the sensation of being full and the burn that was fading to a sweet ache robbed him of his voice. He looked up, met Blake's black eyes with his own heated gaze, and nodded.

Blake groaned and moved, slowly at first, only pulling out slightly before pushing back in deep. "Ah, fuck," he gasped again.

The slow, steady pace didn't last long. It couldn't. Blake grabbed a suspension strap in one hand; the other he wrapped around Ty's cock, pulling him harder onto Blake's thick shaft, and he fucked Ty hard and fast.

His eyes started to roll up, heart hammering in his chest. "Sir… Sir, please, Sir!"

The ring around Ty's cock fell away. "Come for me, Ty. Let me feel you come on me."

"Sir!" Ty screamed as his orgasm ripped through him. White dots danced behind his eyes as he felt the wet heat of his release land on his stomach and chest. He was still coming, only barely aware of Blake slamming into him one last time and roaring his release. Completely spent, Ty relaxed into the swing, let it hold him, melted into it. He was floating again and stopped thinking beyond the warm sated feeling surrounding him. With a smile on his face, Ty closed his eyes. He trusted that Blake would watch over him, care for him, bring him back again.

CHAPTER
SEVENTEEN

FOR the third morning in a row, Ty woke with Blake's heat next to him and opened his eyes to find Blake staring down at him. A smile curled the cowboy's lips when he saw Ty open his eyes.

"Good morning, Ty," Blake murmured, kissing him tenderly on his forehead. "How do you feel?"

Ty said the first thing that popped into his head without thinking. "Amazing." He beamed, shifting and wincing at the stab of pain in his ass. "Sore, well-fucked, but amazing."

"Bad sore?" Blake asked, concerned.

Leaning up, Ty took his own kiss before saying, "Nope. Good sore. But I hope you don't expect me to ride or muck stalls." He chuckled. His ass had a sweet, good kind of aching throb, but if he had to do any kind of heavy chores, it would quickly move into the bad sore.

"Riding and mucking stalls?" Blake wrinkled his nose in disgust. "I would never ask you to do anything I wouldn't do myself." Blake winked. "Chores-wise, that is."

The cute way Blake looked with his nose wrinkled made Ty laugh. "Well I know you ride, but you don't muck stalls? What kind of cowboy are you?"

"The smart kind. Besides, I'm a ranch owner, not a cowboy," Blake countered.

"City boys." Ty groaned, shaking his head.

"Damn straight, and proud of it. I like my comfortable fifth floor apartment within walking distance of anything and everything I need. Indian food at three a.m., crowded sidewalks, and constant noise." Blake waved a hand at Ty. "Okay, so not so much the noise, but you better count your ass lucky I'm not a *real* cowboy." Blake patted the lucky ass in question, and Ty groaned at the sting and nodded in agreement.

"You know," Ty said, lying back and stretching his arms up over his head, back arching slightly as he stretched, "if my ass was really lucky, you'd lie down, snuggle me, and let me go back to sleep." God, he felt good, and he couldn't think of anything he'd rather do than stay wrapped up in Blake's warmth and enjoy the delicious lingering effects of the intense scene they'd shared the night before.

"You can have an extra ten minutes," Blake murmured, wrapping himself around Ty and nuzzling against the side of his neck. "I need breakfast."

Ty took Blake's heat into him, letting it fill him, comfort him. This was the way he should wake up every morning: a pleasant ache in his ass, a sexy man wrapped around him, and no pressing worries other than what to cook Blake for breakfast. How he could please the man after breakfast. *Four more days.* Well, at least he had that. Three days ago, he had nothing but grief and anger and Quinn's betrayal for company.

Wow, that didn't even hurt. Was he still pissed off at Quinn? Yes! Did he still hate Lorcan? Maybe…? It was hard to dwell on the negative feelings when his body felt so sated.

"Can I ask you something?" he asked, pushing his focus back to the man who was real and warm and in bed next to him.

"Sure," Blake drawled easily.

"Why are you running your daddy's ranch if you like big city living so much? Don't you have anyone else, brothers, sisters, that could run it?" he asked curiously.

"I'm the one and only spawn of Carl Cornelius Henderson the third. Guess I just wanted to right some wrongs the old man had done after hearing what a prick he'd been to the folks around here." A sad tone crept its way into Blake's voice. "Plus, I needed to get out of the city for a while. Take a break, so to speak."

Ty wrapped an arm around Blake, running a hand down his spine, wanting to soothe away the sadness he heard. "Got enough mucking stalls when you were a kid, huh?" he teased, keeping it light, not commenting on Blake's harsh description of his dad or his need for a break.

"I've never mucked a stall, nor do I have any plans to start anytime soon."

"Your dad doesn't sound like that much of a prick if he didn't make you shovel cow shit when you were a kid. Sounds like you were spoiled."

Blake pulled back slightly, laying his head against his pillow, still keeping an arm wrapped around Ty's waist, and met Ty's eyes. "I was spoiled," Blake said seriously. "But not by Carl Henderson. The old man didn't want kids, and I'd only ever met the man face to face a few times while I was growing up. Never stepped foot on this ranch before last year. But he set my mom up in a sweet apartment and paid her a nice monthly income to keep me out of his hair, and yeah, she spoiled me rotten."

To Ty, it didn't sound like a bad setup at all. Sure, it sucked that Blake's dad didn't want anything to do with him, but fuck, Ty would have killed to have at least had a mom. "Your mom sounds great," Ty said enviously. "Your relationship with your dad must have gotten better, yeah? He left the ranch to you."

"It started to get better when I was in college working on my MBA. He started calling periodically." Blake shrugged. "I think the greedy bastard was hoping to get a financial advisor cheap. Then five, maybe six years ago, I came home to a message on my answering machine that said 'I won't have a faggot for a son.'" Blake laughed, and it wasn't full of anger or bitterness like Ty would have thought. "Guess he finally opened the invitation to the coming-out party I had at eighteen."

"You don't sound upset."

"Why should I be, Ty? Would I have liked to have had a dad when I was growing up?" Blake shrugged. "I don't know, since I never felt like I was missing out on anything. I had a great life," Blake said, reaching up and caressing Ty's cheek. "I like who I am, and because the bastard was too lazy to change his will after he disowned me, I get the chance to pay back some of the people he hurt. What's to be upset about?"

Ty pushed into Blake's touch and closed his eyes. "I like your look on things. I wish it was always that easy," he mumbled quietly.

He wished he could look back at his childhood and find the positive like Blake did. Find something about his life with Brian that had made him a better person. Wished he could look at his time with Quinn as a growing and learning experience, but he couldn't. He hated what his parents, their families, had done to him by leaving him on the doorstep of a church when he was three. Not one, not one single person in either his mother or his father's family ever came to look for him. He hated the scars on his back, the black mark on his soul, and his inability to trust enough, to fully submit, that was Brian's legacy. And he hated that Quinn had given him a glimpse of a life he could never have but desperately craved.

"It is that easy," Blake whispered, still caressing Ty's cheek.

Shaking his head, not trusting his voice, Ty turned his gaze away from the dark compassionate eyes. He tried to focus on the pillow under Blake's head, on the headboard, anywhere but those searching eyes.

"Look at me, Ty."

Ty shook his head again, keeping his eyes averted. Then Blake cupped his chin, his solid grip hard against his skin. "Focus right here on me. Look at me and tell me what is running through that gorgeous head of yours."

And just like that, while he looked into the warm, dark eyes of Blake Henderson, a crack appeared in the dam that held back all of Tyler Callahan's memories and unwanted emotions. The small crack grew until it couldn't contain the onslaught of rushing events in his life, each wanting to be the first out of the new opening. With one last shuddering breath, the dam burst and Ty relived the hell that had been his life.

He told Blake about having no memories before age three but that he knew from the social workers that he'd been left on the steps of a church. When he started he had been able to hold it together, speaking in slow sentences with disinterest, and then the words started tumbling out of him faster, in jerky, disconnected sentences.

"I don't really remember the names of the people I lived with when I was really young, but I know there were a lot of them. When I was six, I was living with this family. I don't remember their name either, but I remember their house stunk really badly. It was the first time I remember crying because I had to leave one of the homes. I don't think it was because of the people, since I don't remember their name, so it must have been because they had this house full of cats. Cats in the house, the barn, and kittens, a shitload of kittens. The cutest little things, and I remember crying that I had to leave them. I stayed with the next people for the longest. Jones, I think their name was. Funny thing is, even though I lived with them the longest, I don't remember anything about my time there. Weird, huh? Mr. and Mrs. Ganger were who I lived with when I was eight. They had a big dairy farm, or maybe it was a cattle ranch, I don't know. I just know there were a lot of cows and chickens. I don't think the chickens had anything to do with the cows, but who the hell knows. I didn't stay there very long either. I had a hard time mucking the stalls. I was pretty scrawny and short for my age. I think Mr. Granger wanted older boys to help with the farm or ranch, and he dropped me off downtown.

"The next house was where I found out about being gay, but I already told you about that. Umm… Mrs. Lutz was who I lived with when I was twelve. What a hellhole that place was. She would sit her big fat ass on the couch, watching TV, and I'm pretty sure she took me in to watch all the little kids she had. What a fucking joke. I had to keep the kids in their bedrooms or the backyard, and if they cried, I'd get my ass beat. I tried to tell the lazy bitch that she needed to feed the kids. I got my ass beat again for that. She said it was for being lippy, but I think I got the whipping for interrupting her TV lineup. I ran away a couple times from that place, spent some time in juvie, then got sent back. The last time they sent me back, she took a leather belt to me. She didn't have a good grip on the belt, so the buckle caught me. I got a couple nasty scars on my back as a souvenir.

"Teenage years were pretty much a blur, but a few things stood out, like getting and giving my first blow job, trying to fuck Martin Shultz. That was another fucking joke, and I found out real quick that I was a natural bottom. I don't know how I did it or even why I did it, but I was real good in school. Especially high school, but I never got to finish. Not that it mattered, since I've gotten along pretty good without a diploma. But I remember being pissed at the time when Mrs. Kline came to tell me I'd have to go to a group home. I was pissed that Mr. and Mrs. Johnson couldn't wait two fucking months to kick me out so I could finish high school. I got fifty dollars, a letter from the state of Oklahoma declaring me an adult, and a homeless status for my eighteenth birthday."

Ty was aware that his pillow was damp from tears he didn't remember crying. His breathing was a little fast, and he had a sickening feeling in his gut, but as those dark brown eyes kept staring at him, it was like they were encouraging the flood that was pouring from the dam, and he just kept talking.

"After about a week of sleeping wherever I could find a dry spot and still worrying about how I was going to get to school, panicked I wouldn't be able to catch up on my studies if I missed too much more, I met Brian. Don't ask me his last name, because I don't have a goddamn clue. That should have been a warning whistle right there, that I was following some guy to his house, whose last name I didn't even know. A last name didn't seem important at the time. Still isn't. At the time, I guess the thought of a warm dry bed and someone to talk to seemed more important. So there I was living with this older, big bear of a man. Another thing I don't know and don't care is how old he was. All I know was he was old enough that he shouldn't have been picking up young homeless boys on the street, but fuck, I was grateful he did. Brian introduced me to the lifestyle. Taught me about submitting and walking to heel, how to either muscle through or rise above the pain. I had a pretty sweet setup for a while. Cleaning his house, that's where I learned to cook, too, dressing him, bathing him, and he took care of everything else. I was with him for nearly two years, but the last year was another nightmare I couldn't wake up from.

"I think eventually Brian got bored. He'd find dust where there wasn't any and I'd get punished. Come to think of it, I was punished more than I was disciplined or fucked. Have you ever been made to wear a metal cock cage for a month? I don't suggest you ever try that one on a sub. It was worse than the bullwhip or the shock treatments. About three weeks after the cage was put on, Brian and I were doing edge play, you know, oxygen dep, and I remember thinking at the time, 'I hope he chokes me right over that fucking edge.' Yeah, it was that bad. Then he started bringing home strangers. Young guys. I didn't know any of them. I was usually bound to the wall with a ball gag and just watched him fuck 'em. It got pretty bad after that. It was no longer about submission and pleasure but rape, torture, and humiliation. I ran."

There. He'd done it. Ty felt raw, exhausted, embarrassed, pathetic, but at the same time, even as his tears continued to land on his pillow from his tightly closed eyes, he had this weird buzzing kind of pleasure in his gut. For the first time in his life, he didn't have to push all those horrible events in his life, all those dark thoughts, back behind some kind of mental door and lock it. God, he was so tired, but a good kind of tired. The warm kisses against his forehead, his nose, his cheeks, and the soft comforting sounds coming from Blake felt even better.

"I'm so sorry people treated you like that." More kisses, warm and soft, against each of his eyes, his chin. "Let it go and sleep, and when you wake up, I'll be here. Sleep, Ty."

Ty slept.

CHAPTER
EIGHTEEN

THE rest of the day had been relatively quiet. Ty had been a little skittish when he'd woken the second time, but Blake had kept him busy with meals and chores. He'd also given Ty plenty of opportunity to just be still and reflect on what he'd shared with Blake and how he felt about it. Other than a couple of slight panic attacks and one outburst when Blake had pushed Ty to talk more about how he felt when he finally left Brian, Blake had been able to distract Ty easily, and true to Ty's ADD approach to feelings, he calmed easily, forgetting the outburst and moving on to the next task. This morning, Blake planned to reward Ty for the day before.

Blake let his eyes wander appreciatively down Ty's naked body, spread out before him like a feast. Ty sat on the bathroom counter, legs spread, cock hard and curling up toward his tight belly. Blake's own cock filled and throbbed in response. Tonight he'd push again, but for the moment, it was all about mutual pleasure.

"This is so hot," Ty moaned, spreading his legs a little farther apart.

Blake pushed between those spread legs and tugged Ty close to him. "Going to get a lot hotter," Blake promised and gave the man a hard kiss. Blake's mouth traveled downward, leaving biting kisses along Ty's neck and shoulders. Ty arched hard, pushing against the toothy kisses Blake left against his skin. Sucking hard against the side of Ty's neck, Blake marked the man, drawing the blood to the surface and worrying the area with his teeth. When he pulled back and studied his mark, a brief ache fluttered in his heart, but it was gone before he could understand its cause. Putting the odd feeling out of his head, Blake grabbed the shaving cream from the counter. Ty's gaze was heavy on him as he bent down and kissed the head of the man's straining cock before working the white foamy cream into the curls.

"Cold," Ty complained softly, but his hips pushed forward.

Blake picked up the new razor he'd laid out and swiped it gently against Ty's skin, the short blond curls coming off easily, revealing creamy, pale skin below. Ty watched him as he continued to shave the area, moaning his pleasure. Ty's hips started to thrust just a little. "Careful, Ty," Blake warned. "Thrusting your hips against sharp objects might not be wise."

"Feels good," Ty groaned, but his hips stilled.

Blake made quick but careful work of shaving the rest of Ty's groin, rinsing the last remnants of the shaving cream away with a warm cloth. Blake ran a finger across the pale skin, admiring his handwork. "Looks good," Blake murmured, his voice going deep and husky.

With the threat of nicks from the razor removed, Ty began to thrust his hips gently again, pushing into Blake's touch as he continued to swirl his finger lightly around the bare skin. Ty was such a sensualist, and he responded to the touch, moaning his pleasure, begging for more. How long had it been since anyone had done something just for Ty's pleasure? Ty had shown him that he not only needed but also enjoyed the pain Blake could inflict upon his flesh. Ty needed the structure, the peace he found in submitting, but the man also needed a little tenderness.

Blake wrapped a hand around the thick shaft, pumping it lightly, spreading the leaking precum down the length. "This feel good too, Ty?"

"Ah, God, yes," Ty groaned. "So fucking good."

"Then you're going to love this." Blake took Ty's cock into his mouth, tongue swirling around the plump head. He grinned around Ty's cock at the increased squirming and guttural moans his mouth pulled from Ty as he continued to lick and lap at the sensitive flesh. He pulled the stockier man closer, Blake's hands grabbing the fleshiest part of Ty's ass, kneading and rubbing, occasionally letting his fingers slip down the crease to tease at the tight ring of muscles. His mouth was fierce and unrelenting on Ty's cock.

Ty's hands fisted in Blake's hair, and Blake let the man thrust his hips a few times before he took control again. Sliding his hands forward, Blake grabbed Ty's thighs in a bruising grip, shoving them wider and pinning them to the counter, efficiently stopping the man's movements. Blake then took Ty deep into his throat. The hoarse cry of "Sir!" was a satisfying sound and made Blake's own cock throb and leak in the confines of his jeans. Blake ignored it and continued his sensual assault on the warm flesh against his tongue.

Ty's shaft was leaking a steady stream against Blake's tongue. The man's flavor was bitter and musky, and Blake savored it.

"Sir... fuck... Sir... Sir... so close...." Ty cried out above him, his hands fisting tighter in Blake's hair.

Ignoring the pain of Ty's hands being ripped from his hair, Blake surged to his feet, taking Ty's mouth in a fierce and possessive kiss. He wrapped his fist around Ty's near-to-bursting shaft and pulled hard, licking and biting at Ty's mouth. His hand tightened around the flesh in his palm. "Come for me, Ty," he demanded. "Give it to me, now!"

Ty's hips snapped once, his head falling back and eyes rolling up. Ty's mouth went wide in a brief silent scream as heat fountained over Blake's hand and the man's breath rushed out of him. He cried out "Sir!" as his body jerked and convulsed with the force of his release.

Blake continued to stroke Ty through his orgasm, gentling his strokes, bringing Ty down slowly. Then Ty collapsed against Blake, his arms going tightly around Blake, and he began to sob softly against Blake's neck. "So good. So good to me, Sir."

Blake wiped a hand on the towel next to him, then pulled Ty from the counter, holding most of his weight as he steered them toward the master bedroom. Ty clung to him, whimpering and thanking Blake over and over and over. Pulling back the coverlet on the bed, Blake eased them both down onto the bed, surrounded Ty with the heat of his body, and let Ty cling to him.

AFTER an afternoon of heavy submission and a scene that left Ty's back, ass, and thighs red and aching, Blake wrapped Ty in a blanket on the couch in his office to rest while he got some work done. He'd been able to clear his schedule and leave the running of the ranch to Jeremy. He'd also given his foreman strict instructions not to disturb him, trusting the man to handle any problems that might arise during the seven days Ty would be with Blake.

The reports and contracts effectively turning the ranch over to Jeremy couldn't wait. Blake had been away from the city long enough, and it was time he got back and started living his life again. He missed the city, his mom, his friends, and his life. The year he'd spent at the Circle H Ranch hiding from the painful memories had been a necessity, one he was sure had saved his sanity. Nevertheless, it was time to go home. It was time to go back, face his demons and nightmares. His eyes wandered from the papers in front of him to the sleeping Ty. What would happen to Ty once he left the ranch at the end of the week? Would he be able to handle his anger, or would it still consume him? Another question niggling at the back of Blake's mind was why did his chest tighten and his stomach roll with nausea at the thought of never seeing Ty Callahan again? Ty needed someone to care about him, to give a shit what happened to him, or the man would eventually fall back into that consuming anger.

A buzz from the drawer of his desk pulled his eyes and his thoughts away from Ty. After pulling open the drawer, Blake took out his cell phone from where he'd stored it once Ty had agreed to stay. He hadn't wanted any interruptions. The small screen displayed Quinn's name. Rising from his chair, Blake stepped out of the office, closing the door quietly behind him before flipping the phone open.

"Hey, Quinn."

"Damn, are you a busy man. I've been trying to reach you for the last couple of days."

Blake went on high alert. He'd given Quinn his number when they'd been working out the details of the settlement, but the man had never called him since the settlement had been finalized. That the rancher had admitted he'd been trying for a couple of days further heightened his concern. "Yeah, I've been a little busy. What's up?" Blake asked curiously.

There was a slight hesitation, and then Quinn asked, "Any chance you've seen Ty Callahan?"

A little startled, Blake looked at the closed door of his office as if the man in question might appear. "What makes you think I know where he is?"

"Well, the offer you threw him before you left the ranch got me thinking maybe he took you up on it." An uncomfortable laugh came through the phone before Quinn continued. "Look, I'm not trying to pry or anything, I'm just worried about him. After you left, he was upset with me and quit. I've tried his house, and no one at the club he hangs out at has seen him."

Blake moved down the hall and into the great room while Quinn talked. He didn't want Ty to overhear him when he responded to Quinn's question. It really wasn't his place to be telling Quinn that Ty had been staying with him, but he hoped he could get a little information on why Ty was so angry at Quinn and Lorcan.

"Yeah, I've seen him," Blake responded when Quinn paused. "In fact, he's still here."

"Thank God," Quinn said in a rush. "I thought he might have gone and done something stupid."

"Like what?" Blake moved to the large windows and looked out over the fields.

"I don't know, but he was really upset when he left."

"About your upcoming wedding?"

"Yeah," came Quinn's sighed reply.

"I know it's probably none of my business, but I care about Ty, and I don't like that he's so distressed."

"Yeah… yeah, that's good that you care about him. Ty needs that," Quinn said earnestly. "He's a really great guy under all that gruff. I wish things could have…." Quinn's voice trailed off, and Blake heard the creak of a leather chair, as if Quinn had leaned back in his office chair.

"Been different," Blake finished for him.

"Not the outcome, no. I won't ever wish Lorcan hadn't come back into my life, not even for Ty. I just wish we could stay friends. He helped me through a really tough time in my life, and I wish I could be there when he needs someone." Quinn huffed out a breath into the phone before he continued. "I wish I hadn't done to him what I did, is all I meant." Quinn's voice was low and full of regret.

Blake moved to his own leather chair, stretching out, and his fingers tapped against the soft leather arm. "What did you do to him that you wish you could take back?"

"I don't know how much I should say about Ty's lifestyle—"

"I met him at The Push," Blake interrupted. He didn't say that it wasn't the first time he'd met Ty. There was no sense embarrassing either Quinn or Ty by mentioning the scene at the pond.

"Yeah? Okay, so then you probably know Ty's a submissive and into pain?"

"Mm-hmm."

Blake could hear a rustling noise, as if Quinn was shifting around in his chair. "I'm not proud of how things started with Ty, and I'm not going to try and justify my behavior. I'm only going to say that I started seeing Ty in some of my darkest days after Lorcan left me."

There was another brief pause, but Blake didn't say anything. He waited patiently, letting Quinn take this at his own pace.

"I'd met Ty once before, right about the same time Lorcan had started working for me. So when I showed up at The Push a few months after Lorcan had gone back to Indiana, I ran into him again. The first night I went to the club, there was a show going on in the club, and… well, I went in one of the back rooms that night and found an outlet for my anger. I never messed with anyone more than once except Ty," Quinn said uncomfortably. "Ty could handle me when I was very angry."

Blake curled his free hand into a fist, the other squeezing the phone so hard he was surprised it didn't snap in two. The idea of Ty being hit in anger was like a physical blow. No one who willingly submitted should ever be hit in anger. Blake had to remind himself that Ty had submitted, had allowed it to happen more than once, and that kept Blake from lashing out at his neighbor. Blake forced himself to relax and asked, "If it was a mutual arrangement, I don't understand how Ty's anger factors in."

"I got drunk one night—"

"You hit him while you were drunk?" Blake growled angrily, sitting upright, body completely tense with fury.

"No!" Quinn shot back quickly. "I would never do that. I went to the club one night soon after Lorcan came back into town. Ty and I had a scene, and then *after*, we got drunk together and I ended up crying on Ty's shoulder, admitting for the first time to anyone, including myself, how Lorcan's leaving had affected me."

Blake relaxed back in his chair.

"After that night," Quinn continued, "we started hanging out more and more. Jess was in the hospital and I was spending my days with Lorcan, helping around Jess's ranch, and my nights with Ty. I thought Ty understood how much I loved Lorcan; I never lied to him about that. Although we were friends, we shared a physical relationship. Ty and I had just started talking about exploring the Dom/sub thing when Lorcan and I.... Look, Blake, I didn't realize Ty felt more for me until after I told him Lorcan and I were back together. I've tried to make things right between us, and I hate that he won't talk to me. Regardless of what he thinks, I care very much about him."

Quinn's frank admission of his and Ty's relationship explained so much. Blake had seen how Ty responded when someone showed him a little care. Had he not witnessed it with his own eyes, he might have been more suspicious of Quinn's story, believing that Quinn had somehow led the man on. Blake scrubbed a hand across his face. "I know that wasn't easy to talk about, but thank you for telling me. It explains a lot."

"I just wanted you to know that I'm no threat to whatever is going on between you and Ty. Ty deserves to have someone care about him, someone who can love him as more than a friend."

"There is nothing going on between us," Blake said, absently rubbing a hand across his chest. "Ty needed someone, and I was there for him. That's all."

"I hope you do better at being his friend than I did," Quinn said softly. "Will you let him know that I called and that his job is still here?"

"Sure, I'll tell him."

"Thanks."

There was a long moment of silence, like each of them wanted to say more but wasn't sure what to say. Finally, Quinn said, "I gotta run, thanks for taking him in. Talk to you later, yeah?"

"Yeah. And Quinn?"

"Yeah?"

"He doesn't hate you. I don't think he is really even that angry at you; it's more that he's envious that Lorcan has someone who loves him the way you do."

"Thanks, Blake. I hope you're right. Talk to you soon."

"Bye."

Blake flipped his phone shut and rested his head back against the soft leather chair. Quinn had made some mistakes, but if Blake was to believe Quinn, and he did, he hadn't intentionally hurt Ty. It sounded as if Quinn genuinely cared about Ty. Hopefully, Ty would eventually realize that. Having that one special person to care about was important, but having friends that cared was just as important. Blake set the phone on the table next to his chair and went to go check on Ty, suddenly needing to see the man.

CHAPTER
NINETEEN

DRESSED in the jeans and T-shirt he'd arrived in, Ty sat on the large king-size bed he'd shared with Blake for the last week. He was ready to go home. He'd kept his word and stayed the entire seven days. It was questionable as to whether he had truly submitted to Blake, but he'd fallen in and out of a comfortable headspace. There had been outbursts, revelations, tears, and laughter, and he'd needed them all. Blake hadn't pushed him past any newfound boundaries, nor had it truly been about mindless submission. A time for introspection—maybe that was how he should look at it.

There hadn't been any one moment he could look back on and say, "That's it, that's when I realized I wasn't mad at Quinn anymore." If he had to choose one thing that had helped the most, oddly enough, it was talking about his life growing up, his time with Brian. So weird that he'd choose that and not the deep submission. He was definitely going to have to give that one some more thought. Even after Blake told him about Quinn calling because the man had been worried about Ty and to let him know his job was waiting, he hadn't had this grand moment of clarity that Quinn was and always had been nothing more than a friend. With everything he'd shared with Blake, he couldn't pinpoint the exact moment when his anger had drained away. It was not one thing but everything. It had taken spending time with Blake to realize it wasn't Quinn he had been in love with but what they had done together. Just like he loved what he and Blake had done together. It was the Dom persona he'd been in love with, not the Dom.

"I thought I smelled smoke."

Ty's head snapped up, and he found Blake leaning casually against the doorframe. "Huh?" he asked, confused.

"You're obviously thinking too hard. Smoke's pouring out of your ears."

"Shut up," Ty growled teasingly. "That's the lingering smell of the toast you burnt this morning."

"Whatever." Blake pushed away from the door and sat next to Ty, bumping their shoulders together. "So you sure I can't talk you into staying for another day or five?"

"Nah," he responded, shaking his head. "Not that the offer isn't tempting, but I need to get back and check on my place, start thinking about looking for a job."

"You're not going to take Quinn up on his offer and go back to work on his ranch?" Blake questioned.

"No. And it has nothing to do with Quinn and Lorcan. I enjoy spending time on a ranch, but I'm more cut out for slinging suds than shoveling shit."

"I can't say as I blame you for choosing suds over shit." Blake chortled. "You going to go back to The Push?"

"Don't know yet," Ty answered honestly. He might have had a few revelations this week, but he still needed a few days to figure out what he was going to do next. He'd spent so many weeks focused on his anger and seeking revenge that without it, he was somewhat lost.

They sat next to each other, Ty staring down at his lap, Blake staring at him. He didn't need to see Blake's eyes; he could feel them boring into him. Picking at a loose thread on his jeans and keeping his eyes down, Ty asked, "Can I ask you something?"

"Sure," Blake said easily.

"How come you never use the term 'boy' or 'pet' like most Doms do?"

"Because you're not my boy, Ty."

Ty looked up and got a brief glimpse of the dark look he'd seen cross Blake's gaze before, but Blake covered it quickly. "For me, that's an endearment for someone who is *my* submissive, my...." Blake's voice trailed off, and he rubbed a hand across his stubbled chin. Ty could see the concentration on the man's face as he carefully thought about his words before speaking again. "There are a lot of people who play in the lifestyle, but for me it *was* a lifestyle. I don't use terms of endearment lightly."

Ty had never really heard it described that way before. He'd always thought Doms used *boy* to make a distinction of who was in control, the same as when he called a Dom Sir. He'd never thought of either title as an endearment or something special. Looking at it that way, Ty realized sadly that he'd never truly been anyone's boy.

"Did it bother you that I called you 'Sir'?" Ty asked, trying to understand.

"No. Not at all. I know it may sound like a double standard, but I think of the word 'Sir' as a show of respect toward someone in a position of authority, much like you would an officer of the law or a judge, but 'boy' is different. I don't know, Ty. It's just how I look at the word, I guess."

"I can respect that. I was just curious is all." Ty shifted uncomfortably, still picking at the loose threads. "Can I ask you another question?"

Blake put his hand over Ty's, stopping his nervous movements. "You can ask me anything."

Ty looked up and met Blake's gaze. "When I first got here, you explained that you invited me to stay because you'd seen what jealousy could do, and that the anger that stemmed from jealousy could destroy the lives of others. What did you mean when you said you'd seen it?"

"I lost someone I cared about a great deal to jealousy and the anger that grew from it," Blake said sadly.

"Eli?"

Blake nodded slowly, his hand tightening around Ty's. The pain and heartbreak were evident in Blake's chocolate-brown eyes, but he didn't speak.

"What happened to him?"

Patting Ty's hand before standing, Blake turned away from him, moving to the small window and looking out. Ty watched him with concern and wished he hadn't asked the question. "I'm sorry," Ty said softly. "It's none of my business."

"It's okay," Blake said without turning from the window. "I'm just not ready to talk about that right now. Maybe I never will be."

Ty stood and walked over to where Blake stood and placed a hand on the man's shoulder lightly. "I'm grateful for what you did for me this week. And if you ever need to talk, I'd love to repay the favor."

"Thank you."

Ty squeezed Blake's shoulder gently. "Anger isn't the only thing that can destroy someone," Ty whispered.

WAITING until he heard Ty's step moving down the hall before letting out the breath he was holding, Blake fought to keep his emotions under control. Fuck, he hated it when memories of Eli crashed down on him when others were around. He'd lived a lifestyle that dictated he always be in control of himself and others. This new life, this fucking new life of being weak and out of control, was killing him. Ty had given him a glimpse of what he'd had, what he'd been, and dammit, what he wanted to be again. Blake rubbed absently at the ache in his chest, leaning his head back against the wall, and closed his eyes. *I was right, Eli. Ty is a good man, and I think I helped him. He calls to something in me, made me feel again.* Blake opened his eyes and stared at the ceiling, but he was seeing beyond the room. He looked past the plaster and wood and whispered, "But I'm not ready to let you go. I can't."

Pushing away from the wall, Blake ran his hands through his hair. He'd thought coming here to this backward country town would give him a chance to let the past go. He'd righted some wrongs his prick for a father had inflicted on the town of Pegasus. He'd buried the son of a bitch, and hopefully with that he had given a chance for people like Quinn to live their lives without the nefarious legacy of Carl Henderson the third. He'd also gotten a chance to move out of the city where the cafés, theaters, restaurants, parks, street corners, hell, the city itself reminded him of Eli. Blake had brought his memories with him, but he'd been dealing with them. That was, until Ty Callahan decided to do a little peeping Tom. "You may have helped, but at what price?" he asked himself angrily. He'd stopped Ty from doing something stupid, something he'd regret, but in the process, he'd reminded himself what he'd lost and what he could never have again.

Oh, for fuck's sake, enough of the goddamn violins.

He'd done what he'd set out to do in Pegasus, had the added bonus of helping out Ty, and the ranch would soon be turned over to his foreman. Time to head back to the city and—he wasn't sure what he planned on doing once he got back, only that he was done with this country bumpkin town.

Ty was pulling his boots on when Blake made it out to the great room, his emotions under control enough he could walk Ty out to his truck without too much difficulty. "I can't believe you're not going to wait until after lunch. Leave me to make my own sandwich," Blake joked.

"I'm sure you'll manage." Ty finished pulling on his boots, but he didn't immediately move toward the door. Instead, he stood staring at Blake, jingling the keys in his hand nervously.

"It's not about managing, it's about taste. Your sandwiches taste better."

Ty started cracking up. "Oh my fucking God, are you spoiled. It's about throwing some meat, cheese, and mayo between two pieces of bread. The taste doesn't change whether it's me or you slapping it together."

The sound of Ty's laughter did Blake's heart good, helping to push the morose feeling farther down. The smile on the man's face that followed the laughter helped keep those feelings down. Ty was stunning when he smiled. "The taste might not change, but watching you moving around the kitchen while you make it, yum!"

The pink blush to Ty's cheeks was adorable. The cowboy didn't do so well with compliments, at least not outside of the bedroom. Before Blake could think better of it, he grabbed onto Ty's shirt near his waist with both hands and pulled Ty against him. "You going to come back and make me lunch again sometime?"

Ty looked a little stunned for a moment, but he didn't try to pull away. Rather, Blake could feel the man pushing against him. "Not sure, cowboy. You gave me a lot to think about, lots to digest, ya know?"

"Yeah, I know. Just be careful you don't think too hard. Don't want you keeling over from smoke inhalation."

Ty laughed again at the old joke and then grew serious, his hands moving to wrap around Blake's waist. "It's been a good week, Blake. I know at times I was a prick, and at others pretty fucking pathetic, but you really helped give me a chance to clear my head. Thank you."

"You were never pathetic, Ty," Blake assured him. "A little scared, a little lost, and at times a whole lot of pissed off, but never pathetic."

The pink color of Ty's cheeks deepened to a darker hue as they continued to stare at each other. Ty still seemed a little apprehensive, twitchy, but the man looked good. A new air seemed to have fallen over Ty. Gone was the fake cockiness, replaced with, if not peace, then at least a hint of what the man would be like once he found it. Not one for long drawn-out goodbyes, Blake leaned in and kissed Ty softly on the cheek.

"Take a couple of days and get your head on straight, then give me a call and let me know how you're doing, okay? Or, if you need someone to talk to while you're getting your head on straight, I'm here to listen."

Ty surprised him by kissing Blake fully on the mouth, his lips warm and insistent, and Blake opened his mouth and let Ty's seeking tongue in. Blake didn't try to take control of the kiss, let Ty take from it what he needed and take it where he wanted it to go. Blake's shaft began to fill as Ty's tongue slid along his own, the man's flavor rich and strong in his mouth. God, he wanted to shove Ty up against the wall, dominate the kiss and the stocky body in his arms, but Blake held back.

Ty moaned into the kiss, the sound vibrating against Blake's tongue, going straight to his groin. Ty didn't deepen the kiss, but he explored Blake's mouth thoroughly but tenderly, leaving them both breathing a little hard and Blake panting when the kiss ended. Kissing his way across Blake's cheek until his lips were against the sensitive skin below Blake's ear, Ty murmured, "And you have my number if you need someone to talk to as well." Ty laid one last kiss on Blake's neck, then pulled away.

Ty, obviously not one for long goodbyes either, opened the door and stepped out. "See ya around, cowboy," Ty called out as he moved toward his old truck without looking back.

Stepping out onto the porch, Blake watched Ty climb into his truck and pull out of the drive without a wave or a backward glance. Blake stared at the drive long after the dust Ty's truck had kicked up settled. An empty feeling even more profound than normal settled into Blake's gut as he continued to stare at the now-empty road. The ranch around him was busy with activity. He could hear some of the hands laughing from the direction of the barn, others yelling orders, and still more cussing at animals who dared to ignore their commands. However, for some reason, he felt completely alone. Blake looked up at the cloudy morning sky. Off in the eastern distance, dark clouds were moving in fast. A hell of a storm was brewing. It seemed fitting, since a storm was brewing in Blake's gut too.

"What do you think, Eli? Think Ty is going to be okay?"

He nodded and headed back to the house as the sun peeked out briefly from behind the clouds. "Yeah, I think he's going to be okay too."

CHAPTER
TWENTY

MAN JAILED FOR LIFE FOR TORTURE, RAPE AND MURDER

Pond Pleasant Independent News

A man obsessed with violent BDSM was told he must spend the rest of his life in jail today after admitting to the horrific kidnapping, torture, rape, and murder of Eli Gonzalez.

Unemployed John Wood, 38, drugged and kidnapped Gonzalez, 27, taking him to Wood's home and acting out his sick fantasies, inflicting horrific sexual injuries before stabbing him and strangling him with a guitar string.

He carried out the attack on the afternoon of April 3 and took Gonzalez to his home in Saginaw, New York, where he kept Gonzalez chained in his basement for approximately four days.

Wood was obsessed with Gonzalez, having harassed the Pond Pleasant man for months. The day before Gonzalez was kidnapped, a restraining order was issued in Genesee County, prohibiting Wood from coming within 500 yards of Gonzalez.

From Wood's computer, police recovered a folder of bondage, rape, and torture entitled "For My Boy Eli."

Passing sentence, Genesee County Judge Anthony said that in this case the mandatory sentence of life without parole for aggravated murder is completely appropriate—and he will never be released.

The judge also said: "The terror, the unimaginable pain, and the indignities Wood inflicted on Mr. Gonzalez... this was a horrific crime in which a young man who had everything to live for had his life cut short. It was premeditated, and his agony must have been prolonged.

"This is one of those exceptional cases in which the only just punishment requires you to be imprisoned for the rest of your life."

Speaking after the case, Gonzalez's partner, Blake Henderson, said: "Eli was my best friend. He was always happy. He brought a smile to everyone he met. Eli was loved by everyone who was blessed to know him. Eli wasn't just my partner, he was my everything.

"Not a day goes by when I don't think of him. I love and miss him so much and always will."

Detective Chief Inspector David Jones, who led the investigation for Pond Pleasant Police, said: "This is a case of envy and jealousy that led to murder.

"He was so jealous of the relationship between Mr. Henderson and Mr. Gonzalez that he caused suffering not only to Eli but also to his family and those who cared about him.

"He will now have a long time to reflect on what he has done."

Earlier, prosecutor Michael Cole, criminal district attorney, told the court Gonzalez was murdered not only out of jealousy but so Wood could act out his perverted fantasies.

In a drawer of Wood's desk, police found stories taken from something called the "Torture Bondage Handbook."

Both Gonzalez and Henderson were frequent patrons of a known BDSM club called The Whip, located in the fourteenth block of Lennon Avenue, which Wood also frequented. According to the owner, who wishes to remain unnamed, "Blake and Eli had a long-term, consensual, and loving relationship that Wood was jealous of."

Gonzalez was taken to Wood's home on April 3 just before 3:00 p.m. Wood was then free to act out his "sexual fantasy" to torture and rape, which lasted for four days.

In a dark room in the basement, Gonzalez was found lying face-up, bound to a table, naked apart from a pair of socks, and clearly dead.

Near his body were two knives, a broom handle, and a variety of sex toys, all stained with Gonzalez's blood.

A postmortem examination revealed that Gonzalez had been sodomized and suffered severe internal injuries, some of which had been inflicted while he was still alive.

His injuries led to severe blood loss, but the predominant cause of death was ligature strangulation.

Gonzalez's partner and other family members wept silently, heads bowed and covering their faces with their hands as the details were given to the court.

Wood was arrested and later told police, "I only wanted him to love me back" but admitted to the rape and murder of Gonzalez.

Wood, dressed in a black shirt, paisley tie and tan jacket, sat impassively in the dock as details of the injuries he inflicted on Gonzalez were read out in court.

He made no reaction as he was told he must spend the rest of his life behind bars.

TY SWALLOWED down the bile that had risen up in his throat and wiped at the tears that had dampened his cheeks as he read what had happened to Blake Henderson's partner, lover, and *boy*. A picture of Blake and Eli accompanied the news article. Blake had his arm around a smaller, very handsome man, and both men had huge smiles on their faces. Another photo showed a man, his face hidden in his hands. Ty recognized Blake by the dark black hair and body type. Numerous other people who Ty assumed were Eli's family and friends also had their heads bowed, their faces hidden in their hands. A few looked straight ahead with horror-stricken expressions on their faces. A third photo was a picture of a dark dungeon of a room. An examination table stood in the middle of the room, shackles hanging from all four corners, and numerous weapons and implements were mounted to the wall. The caption read "The dungeon where Eli Gonzalez was held for four days." Looking at the room where Blake's lover had suffered and ultimately been tortured to death was too much, and with a shaking hand, Ty slammed down the lid on his laptop.

"Your anger has nothing to do with Eli, but I've seen what jealousy can do. Jealousy clouds your judgment, and you will end up

doing things you'll regret. Thing you can't ever take back. It will eventually destroy you, and anger that stems from that jealousy can destroy the lives of others."

Blake's words came back to Ty. He'd thought Blake was talking about a relationship ending and not being able to get over being dumped, but the truth… fuck, the truth was so much more horrible than he could have ever imagined, ever wanted to imagine. Was that where Ty had been headed before Blake intervened? He knew he would never torture or rape Lorcan, but would he have killed him if his anger were left to fester long enough?

Ty barely made it to the bathroom before he vomited when his own words came back to him. *"Or so help me God, I will fucking kill him!"*

Long after his stomach was empty, his gut continued to wretch and heave as he remembered how black and ugly his anger had become. How close—

"No! Please, God… no… I wouldn't have killed him," Ty cried in between the dry heaves wracking his belly.

Ty's stomach continued to roll and twist as sobs poured from his soul. His mind tormented him with images; Eli's smiling face, the room he had been tortured in, and Lorcan's face flashed through his mind. How long Ty continued to anguish over what he could have done he didn't know, but when the wracking sobs finally quieted and his stomach decided it wasn't worth it, Ty was left wrung out and clinging to the porcelain bowl, but even exhausted, he knew what he had to do.

After rinsing his mouth and washing his face, Ty left the bathroom and grabbed his phone from the table next to the couch. Flipping it open, he hit speed-dial #1.

"Can I come over, please?" Ty begged as soon as the phone stopped ringing.

"Sure, are you okay?"

"No. I'll see you in a little while." Ty didn't wait for a response. He closed the phone, shoved it into his front pocket, and grabbed his keys from the table.

HEART hammering in his chest, Ty wiped his sweaty palms on his jeans and knocked on the door. Adrenaline was surging through his system, and he wanted nothing more than to give in to the flight response screaming at him to run, but he held his ground.

"C'mon in," Quinn said with a smile as he held the door open to Ty.

"Thanks," Ty said gratefully. One more minute and the run response might have won out.

Ty stepped into Quinn's living room, unable to meet the man's eyes. "Um… any chance Lorcan is here?"

Quinn shut the door and waved him toward the couch, "Yeah, he's in the back room. He wanted to give us a little privacy to chat."

Ty bypassed the couch and sat in one of the recliners, still not meeting Quinn's eyes. "Would you mind asking him to join us? What I have to say… what I need to tell you involves him as well."

Quinn hesitated, and Ty could feel the man's eyes on him. "You okay, Ty?" Quinn asked, concerned.

Nodding, Ty responded, "I'm okay, now. Just a couple of things I need to get off my chest, to both of you." Ty looked up and met Quinn's eyes briefly before looking away, unable to stand the concern in Quinn's eyes. He didn't deserve Quinn's worry, and Ty would be lucky if that concern didn't end up turning into rage and he didn't have to take his kicked ass home. It was nothing less than he deserved. Sighing, Ty muttered, "Please."

"Yeah, hold on, I'll go get him. You want a drink or something? You look like you could use a beer, maybe something a little stronger?"

"Nah, I'm good, but thanks."

"Okay, be right back."

Ty pulled in a deep breath through his nose and let it out slowly through his mouth. His hands were now not only damp but also shaking like crazy, and he tucked them under his thighs. His gut clenched, threatening to start its heaving again when he realized what he was about to admit to. His ass being kicked wasn't the only thing he had to worry about—his kicked ass could end up in jail.

Too bad. Time to man up, and if you end up in jail, it will be because you deserve it, a little voice he supposed was his conscience whispered to him. And, of course, it was right.

"Hi, Ty. Quinn said you wanted to talk to us," Lorcan greeted him, coming into the room holding hands with Quinn.

Ty smiled when seeing their hands entwined didn't send him into a fit of rage like it would have a week ago. "Would you mind having a seat? Might give me a chance if you're sitting*." A chance to run, that is.*

Once Quinn and Lorcan were seated, Ty finally found the last stores of his courage, lifted his head, and looked them both in the eyes. "I left the messages about Jess and The Push, and I also broke into Quinn's room and messed with your watch, Lorcan," Ty said in a rush. "I'm really sorry. I was pissed and jealous and… and I have no good excuse for what I did. I can only say I'm sorry." Ty braced himself and waited for what was to come.

Quinn stiffened, but Lorcan laid a hand on Quinn's lap and addressed Ty. "I suspected it was you. I'm not going to lie, the messages you left hurt, and I spent many hours questioning myself because of them. But," he continued softly, "I also tried to understand what you were going through and never told Quinn of my suspicions. I knew you loved him and he loves you too, so I kept hoping eventually you two would work it out."

"No, he doesn't—"

"It's okay, Ty," Lorcan interrupted. "I know Quinn loves you, and I'm okay with it, because he loves you as a friend."

Ty swallowed hard to dislodge the lump that formed in his throat at the compassion Lorcan was showing him. He didn't deserve it.

"It's true," Quinn added. "I do love you as a friend. I've been trying to tell you that for weeks, but you wouldn't listen. I've also been trying to tell you that you helped me through a very rough time in my life, and for that I'll always be grateful to you. I don't say this to hurt you, but had it not been for you helping me past my anger, offering me a shoulder to cry on, I never would have become the man Lorcan could marry." Quinn smiled at Lorcan, and the smile was still there when he turned back to Ty. "You are one stubborn son of a bitch, Ty."

"I overheard Clint talking about the cameras you had installed. I'll pay for any expenses," Ty offered pathetically.

"Oh, you did us a favor there." Lorcan laughed. "Jake's boy installed some cameras he had laying around, and Quinn got the gutters cleaned for free."

"Blay was pissed. Poor kid had to get his hands dirty." Quinn laughed.

Ty scrubbed a hand over his face. This was too easy, and he didn't know if he could trust what they were saying or if he was dreaming. "That's it? You're both just going to accept my apology just like that?"

"Oh trust me, Ty, I planned on kicking the ass of whoever it was that put sadness in Lorcan's eyes, and I'm a little disappointed I don't get to avenge my man's honor." Quinn chuckled when Lorcan swatted his leg. "Okay, okay," Quinn said, properly chastised, and rubbed his leg. "I'm just glad it's over and it wasn't someone truly twisted." He arched a brow at Ty. "Well, any more twisted than you."

"So that's it? All is forgiven and forgotten?" Ty asked incredulously.

"As hard as it was, Quinn and I also learned that nothing was going to come between us. Our relationship passed its first test." Lorcan shot a quick look at Quinn before continuing. "Okay, so maybe our second test. The point is, it did strengthen our relationship, and I think it helped Quinn to ask me to marry him even sooner than he would have."

"I would have eventually," Quinn said sincerely, entwining his fingers with Lorcan's.

"Can I ask you one thing, though?" Lorcan asked.

"Anything," Ty responded quickly.

"Why the change of heart?" Lorcan asked curiously.

One passage from the article he'd read popped into Ty's head. *He was so jealous of the relationship between Mr. Henderson and Mr. Gonzalez that he caused suffering not only to Eli but also to his family and those who cared about him.* The article may have been what had him picking up the phone and asking Quinn if he could come over; however, it was Blake Henderson that had been the catalyst.

"I wish I could tell you that I finally got my head out of my ass and realized what an idiot I'd been acting like. But I needed someone to help dislodge it. Blake told me that you called," Ty said, addressing Quinn. "Thanks for worrying about me, even after I acted like a dickweed."

"Being a dickweed is part of your charm, Ty, and you're welcome," Quinn said sincerely.

Ty rolled his eyes, relaxing a little at Quinn's ability to joke even after the revelation Ty had just made. "Blake asked me to stay with him—well, more like encouraged me to stay, since he was pretty sure I was the… stalker," Ty said, cringing at the label for what he'd done.

"He blackmailed you?" Lorcan asked, surprised.

"No, he wouldn't do that," Ty instantly defended Blake. "I don't think he would have told either of you, but he would have kept an eye on me. The best way I can describe what happened over the week was, he gave me time to realize what I'd done and what I had become on my own. I finally realized that it wasn't Quinn I was in love with but the Dom—" Ty clamped a hand over his mouth, panicked. He didn't even know if Lorcan knew what all had happened between him and Quinn.

"The Dom persona you fell in love with?" Lorcan finished for him. "I don't know how you met Quinn, and I didn't ask, but Quinn has told me all about how you were there for him and, without the intimate details, about what the two of you shared."

Ty met Quinn's gaze, looking for approval. He sighed in relief and let his hand fall back to his lap when Quinn nodded.

"I didn't realize you knew Blake," Quinn commented.

"I didn't until recently. I ran into him at The Push one night, and let's just say it didn't go well. I'm pretty sure he got a hell of a view of my anger that night. He basically walked out on me and told me to give him a call when I was ready to submit." Ty shrugged toward Quinn. "You saw my response to his proposal the day I quit."

"So what made Blake offer to take you in?" Quinn questioned as he pulled Lorcan closer to his side, both men getting comfortable on the couch.

Ty had to admit that the strong masculine man looked good with the handsome Lorcan next to him. Another thing he had to admit was Lorcan didn't look pansy or girlish. He was a very beautiful man, but in no way was his beauty feminine. What made them even more perfect next to each other was the obvious love between them, and Ty was even more thankful Blake had intervened before Ty could destroy it. Was he still jealous? Oh hell yeah, he was jealous, but only because he hadn't found what they had for himself.

"My anger," Ty admitted.

"There has got to be more than that," Lorcan said, puzzled.

"He didn't want to see what happened to Eli ever happen again."

"Eli?" Quinn asked, confused.

"You don't know what happened to his partner? I would have thought.... You've known him for quite a while. I just figured you'd know since you two are neighbors and all."

Quinn shifted and looked uncomfortable before admitting in a low voice, "I met him when he offered to pay the settlement. I was pretty much a wreck back then. I'm embarrassed to admit that it's only been recently that I've really gotten to know him. Hell, I didn't even know old man Henderson had a kid until I met Blake."

"Yeah, he told me Henderson didn't want a kid. Long story, but Blake had never been to the ranch until after his old man died."

"What happened to his partner?" Lorcan asked.

Ty couldn't bear to repeat what he'd read. "Hold on," he said softly. Pulling out his cell phone, Ty quickly found the webpage with the news article he'd read and handed it to Quinn.

He watched both Quinn and Lorcan closely, knew each line they were reading by the looks on their faces: shock, repulsion, grief, and then disbelief.

"Dear God," Lorcan groaned and buried his face against the neck of a stone-faced Quinn, who stared at a spot behind Ty's shoulder.

After what felt like an eternity, Quinn, without meeting Ty's eyes, asked, "Would you have hurt him?"

Ty didn't need to ask whom. From the look on Quinn's face, Ty was sure Quinn was putting himself in Blake's shoes. "I would never have done those things, but would I have hurt him?" Ty hung his head in shame. "I don't know," he answered honestly.

When a hand landed on Ty's shoulders a few moments later, he was shocked to look up and see Lorcan standing over him holding out Ty's cell phone. Ty accepted it, gripping it tightly in his hand.

"Thank you for being honest, Ty. I know that couldn't have been easy."

"I hate that it's true. I'm so sorry," Ty whispered, his voice cracking as he lowered his head again.

Quinn's hands landed on Ty's knees. When he met Quinn's eyes, there was a fierceness in them. "Then I owe Blake for a hell of a lot more than settling a little claim. He may have saved not only the man I love, but also my friend."

When Quinn grabbed Ty, pulling him forward in the chair and into a tight bear hug, Ty had to fight back the tears. Quinn had forgiven him, and the extra hand against his back told him Lorcan had too.

CHAPTER
TWENTY-ONE

THE heavily weighted paper imprinted with elegant script on the counter gave Blake the perfect excuse to call the man who had been on his mind for the last three days. Ty had needed some time to come to terms with what he'd discovered about himself during the week they had spent together, but Blake was becoming increasingly impatient. Convincing himself it had nothing to do with missing the stocky cowboy and everything to do with the invitation, he opened his cell phone and dialed Ty's number. He only wanted to make sure Ty was okay, that the man hadn't fallen back into grief or, more importantly, anger when he received his invitation.

"Hello?"

It's just a checkup call, he warned his heart when it started to beat a little faster the second he heard Ty's voice. "I was just wondering what you made for breakfast?"

"What?"

Blake leaned back against the kitchen counter and sipped his coffee, his throat suddenly dry. "I had toast."

"Did you burn it again?" Ty laughed, the happy sound of it settling right in the center of Blake's chest.

"I didn't burn it, the toaster did," Blake countered. "But as I was eating my crispy toast, I was thinking pancakes with berries and whipped cream sure would be good this morning."

"If it makes you feel any better, I had a stale granola bar this morning."

"No, now I'm even more depressed that we both had horrible breakfasts when I know this really great cook who can make a mean pancake."

"Such a tragedy." Ty snickered.

"It is."

There was an awkward pause, and Blake glanced over at the invitation before asking, "How are you doing, Ty?"

"I'm good. I went and saw Quinn and Lorcan yesterday."

"Wow. How did that go?" Blake was pleased that his voice sounded even, no traces of the shock he felt.

"I told them it was me that left the messages. It was hard, but good, ya know?"

"Yeah?" Blake asked cautiously. He wished he could have been there when Ty had confessed to Quinn and Lorcan. Held his hand.

"Yeah. I think Quinn wanted to beat my ass when I first told him. I mean, I can't really blame him after the way I upset Lorcan, but he forgave me."

"And Lorcan?"

"Surprisingly, it was Lorcan that forgave me the easiest." There was such remorse in Ty's voice when he continued that Blake wanted to wrap his arms around the man and comfort him. "Lorcan is a really great guy… I can't believe how I treated him… the things I thought about him."

"Ty, they forgave you, now you have to forgive yourself. Yes, it's true you did a crappy thing to them, but you manned up to your mistakes and apologized before it went too far."

"I'm working on it. Thanks."

Blake set down his coffee mug and picked up the invitation. "Ty?"

"Yeah?"

"I got an invitation today—"

"To the wedding?" Ty interrupted. Ty sounded okay with it, no trace of sadness and, more importantly, no anger.

"Are you going to go? If you were thinking about it, I was kind of hoping you and I could go together."

"The wedding is in ten days, Blake."

"Not enough time to get a dress?"

"Shut up," Ty teased easily. "I only meant that, yeah, I'm going to the wedding, so we can hang out, only that it's in ten days."

Still not clueing in to what the hell Ty was implying, Blake threw the invitation back on the counter and rubbed at the back of his head. Ty hadn't committed to going to the wedding with Blake, but he hadn't said no either.

"I was thinking ten days is an awful long time." Ty's voice took on a lower tone. "Maybe I could make you pancakes sometime, you know, while we're waiting for the big day."

Blake's body heated with the seductive lilt in Ty's voice. His cock, which had been half-hard since he'd first heard Ty's voice, filled rapidly. "I like pancakes for dinner too," Blake responded with a bit of seduction in his own voice.

"What a coincidence. I was making pancakes for dinner tonight."

Blake pressed his hand against the bulge in his jeans, trying to ease the ache. Fuck, he missed Ty. "Is that an invite?" he asked, hopeful.

"Six o'clock."

"I'll be there." Blake ended the call without saying goodbye, his breath a little too quick. There was no reason to let Ty know how eager he was or just how much the man affected him.

SHEETS cleaned, furniture polished, and floor vacuumed, Ty looked around his small home in disgust. The house was clean, but no matter how you polished it, it was still a shithole. But when he opened the door, all worries of what Blake would think of the house were gone. Standing on the other side of the door in dark jeans and a pale yellow T-shirt, looking delicious, was Blake, thrusting a bottle of maple syrup at him. Ty burst out laughing at the image of the sexy Dom standing with sweet syrup in his hand.

"What?" Blake smiled. "I wanted to make sure you had enough. I thought of bringing a can of Reddi-wip but figured that might look a little too eager."

Ty took the syrup and ushered Blake in, shutting the door behind him. "Or hopeful and horny." He snorted. "You know, most guys bring alcohol in hopes of getting lucky. Gotta say, you're the first to bring me syrup."

"I like being different," Blake admitted with a shrug.

"You are that," Ty muttered. The man was definitely different from anyone Ty had ever met. "Come on in, I was just getting ready to heat up the griddle. Can I get you something to drink?"

A beer would be nice right about now, help with the jittery feeling in his gut, but Blake didn't drink, so Ty had stocked the fridge with pop and juice. Ty was also hoping Blake would be staying for dessert, and he didn't want alcohol clouding any of his later memories. They might come in handy on those long nights when he was alone.

Blake stopped Ty's movement toward the kitchen with a hand on Ty's arm. He tugged and took the bottle of syrup from Ty with his other hand, setting it on the table next to the couch. "I've been worried about you," Blake admitted. "I want to hear how you've been first." Blake urged Ty to the couch and wrapped an arm around Ty's shoulders.

Christ, he'd missed Blake's heat against him, his hands on him. Ty took a moment to savor the feel of Blake next to him before speaking. "I've been good. Had a lot to come to terms with, apologize for. I'm still confused about a few things, but for the most part, I feel really good for the first time in a very long time."

"Still confused about what?" Blake asked, massaging a hand down Ty's arm. The touch was tender, and Ty pushed into it.

"What I want, where I'm going to go from here, you know, those kinds of things."

"Have you decided what you're going to do for work? Sometimes keeping busy while working through things helps," Blake suggested.

"Not yet, but I'll make a decision about that soon. What about you, Blake? How have you been?"

Ty wasn't going to tell Blake that he'd read the news article about Eli and that he knew how his lover had died. He'd seen the agony in Blake's eyes and didn't want to make the man relive that horrifying event in his life. He'd had a lot of time to think back on what he'd done to Quinn and Lorcan, what factors had played into his anger and, more importantly, time to think about how he wanted to live the rest of his life. Ty still held a deep resentment for how his parents and their families had abandoned him and anger at what his life was like as a young child. Those things he still hadn't come to terms with, but he was dealing with them, not ignoring the feelings the memories stirred in him anymore. Funny how Blake had helped him set aside his anger long enough so that he could look at the causes of the ugly emotions corrupting his judgments, and yet, Blake hadn't set aside his grief long enough to look at it, deal with it, and move on. The agony Ty had seen in Blake was proof that the man hadn't taken the advice he'd given to Ty.

"This is about you and how you're doing, remember?" Blake pointed out. "Though I will admit, I've been kind of cranky lately. No one to make me breakfast." Blake shifted, resting his free hand on Ty's thigh. "No one to share a hot bath with." The hand on Ty's thigh tightened, setting Ty's nerve endings ablaze with desire. Blake then leaned in and whispered against Ty's ear, "No one to share my bed with."

Ty shuddered. He'd tried to put his attraction to Blake aside while he dealt with everything else in his head, but it came back in a rush with the warm breath on his neck and the strong hand stroking his thigh. "Did you come here under the pretense of wanting pancakes in order to seduce me?" Ty asked, his voice husky with arousal, and he tipped his head to the side, giving Blake better access.

"No," Blake murmured between soft kisses and nips of his teeth. "I'm here because I missed you." Blake's mouth hesitated against Ty's neck, as if the admission had shocked him. Then he groaned as if he were helpless against the admission and attacked Ty's neck with fierce possessive kisses, startling and slightly frightening in their intensity. The hand on Ty's thigh began to explore frantically. "Jesus, I missed you. What did you do to me, Ty?"

Ty had no clue what he'd done to Blake to make him react so powerfully, but Ty was incapable of fighting it. A sudden flare of desire shot through him, and Ty groaned, turning his head, needing to feel Blake's mouth on his. As Blake devoured his mouth, Ty's body arched into the warm hand that had moved up from his thigh and was now roughly rubbing and pinching at his nipples. Shockwaves of stinging, painful jolts shot directly to Ty's now-aching cock.

Clothes began to fall away in a crazed frenzy of hands pulling and tugging, their mouths rarely losing contact until they were naked, skin touching from head to toe, with the dominant Blake on top.

Blake pulled back to look down at Ty, whose breath was coming in short pants, mirroring his. "Want you." Blake's eyes were hooded and his voice low and sultry, making Ty's stomach flutter.

Ty groaned and arched his back, completely at the mercy of the husky sound of Blake's demanding words and the strong body pressed hard against his own. Blake then threaded his fingers in Ty's hair, tugging his head to the side, and leaned down, sucking hard at the large tendon on the side of Ty's neck. A thrill rocketed down Ty's spine as the pressure of Blake's mouth increased.

Ty's hard shaft rocked into Blake's stomach, and he gave in to the consuming need, bucking against the hard ridge of muscles. "Fuck!" Ty grunted, his hips snapping, causing a delicious friction against the entire length of his cock. Blake pressed his free hand down hard on Ty's bucking hips, pinning him to the couch and restricting Ty's movements with his weight and hand, continuing to suck and nip at the side of Ty's neck. Just as one spot began to burn almost painfully, Blake would move to the other.

Blake was slowly tormenting him, and Ty was panting and moaning, unable to move. He could only whimper as he endured the erotic pleasure of Blake's mouth and heated body pressed against him. The throbbing in his groin grew, turning into an inferno of heat. Ty began to squirm, gasping as each small movement forced Blake's hard-as-steel erection against Ty's equally hard cock.

The hand in Ty's hair loosened, the strong fingers now massaging instead of pulling, matching the rhythm of the sucking kisses against Ty's neck and collarbone.

"God, you feel good," Blake murmured, shifting between Ty's thighs, forcing them wider apart.

Blake continued his unhurried movements. He trailed warm, wet kisses along Ty's neck, making him jerk when his lips moved over the overly sensitive areas where Blake had marked him. Then Blake moved up, running the tip of his tongue along the shell of Ty's ear, pulling another shudder from Ty, before moving to lick a path along Ty's jaw.

His body trembling with need, Ty hooked his legs around his lover's waist, bringing Blake's erection more firmly against his own. Blake moaned, a deep and rumbling sound from low in his chest that made Ty's cock pulse in anticipation.

When his patient and unhurried lover still didn't take it further, Ty arched hard, straining against Blake's restraining body. "Christ, Blake. Fuck me right now, please!" Ty begged, his body like a live wire, racing toward detonation. He wanted his lover buried deep inside him before the explosion. "Hurry, please!" Ty panted, squeezing his eyes shut as he fought against his impending orgasm.

Abruptly, the hand in Ty's hair was gone and so was Blake's weight against his chest. Ty's eyes flew open, and he tightened the hold he had on Blake by wrapping his legs around the man tighter.

"Shh. It's okay, Ty. Just grabbing a condom, no way am I going anywhere."

Ty relaxed back against the couch, letting his legs fall open, giving Blake room to dig into the pocket of his jeans for lube and a condom. In no time at all, Blake was once again pressing down on Ty, nudging against his entrance.

The frantic pace with which they had stripped off their clothing and the following slow, teasing pace gave way to the perfect rhythm. Each one of Blake's downward thrusts was matched and met with an upward press from Ty. It was unlike any other time they had been together, a slow, gentle buildup. Blake's hands never left Ty's skin, his lips rarely leaving Ty's mouth. It was tender, sweet, and by the time Ty could put a name to their mating, his orgasm was racing down his spine. It wouldn't be denied. Ty cried out his release into Blake's mouth, the man pulling in Ty's sounds and feeding Ty his own as Blake's hips snapped one last time and he followed Ty into orgasm.

Their breathing and heart rates had barely returned to normal when Ty found himself thrown across his bed, and Blake showed Ty just what a demanding and aggressive lover he could be. When it was over, Ty snuggled his aching but sated body closer to Blake's side, trailing his fingers up and down the smooth skin of Blake's chest. The satisfied and spent quiet of the room had an edge to it. A tense, unwanted feeling skirted around them, threatening to destroy the calm.

Blake had been like a man possessed when he fucked Ty into the mattress the second time. Blake wasn't possessed in the sense that he was chasing another mind-blowing orgasm, but rather he had been trying to pound the feelings of their lovemaking out of Ty's thoughts and his own. Blake had let down all his walls, dropped the hard-won control of a Dom, and showed Ty another side of himself, the side of Blake that craved and missed the love that he'd lost. Now the two sides of Blake collided and left him staring blankly at the ceiling above them.

When the silence became palpable, Ty felt it as a sickening churn in his gut. Suddenly uncomfortable lying next to Blake but too afraid to pry, Ty flopped onto his back and mimicked Blake, staring at the ceiling.

Ty had been staring so long at the ceiling that his vision began to swim and he could feel sleep starting to settle in when Blake grabbed his hand and squeezed lightly. Ty turned his head and found Blake still staring at the ceiling, but his brow was now furrowed as if he were concentrating hard.

Not able to stand the silence anymore, Ty finally teased, "Are you going to talk to me, or are you going to leave me hanging, thinking I'm the worst lay you've ever had?" hoping to ease some of the tension in the room.

Blake didn't laugh, nor did he answer the question. Instead he rolled slightly, placed a kiss to Ty's forehead, then muttered, "It's nothing to do with you.... I'm... yeah, I'm going to go."

Ty grabbed Blake's hand, refusing to let him pull away. "That has got to be the shittiest thing anyone could say to a man after he just spent the last two hours with his dick up his ass," Ty snapped crudely.

Blake glared at him. "No, the shittiest thing to say is I just spent the last two hours with my dick up your ass, doing to you what Quinn did, fucking you while my heart belongs to someone else."

The statement was like a sucker punch to Ty's gut, and he released his hold on Blake as if he'd just been burnt. Before he thought better of it, wanting to lash out for the dagger Blake had just thrust in his gut and twisted, Ty growled, "At least Quinn dumped me for someone who loved him back and not a ghost."

Now it was Blake's turn to look as if he'd received a blow, but Ty felt no satisfaction in the retaliation. "Blake, I'm sorry." He reached out to take Blake's hand again, but the man jerked out of Ty's reach, left the bed, and stomped out of the room.

"Fuck!" Ty groaned, rubbing his temples at the sudden painful throb. *Way to go, asswipe, you just threw the man's murdered lover in his face.*

Hurrying from the bed, Ty grabbed a pair of sweats from the dresser, pulled them on, and raced after Blake. Ty found him sitting on the couch, dressed and pulling on his boots. "Please don't go—I'm really sorry. I shouldn't have said that."

Blake finished pulling on his boots, rubbed his hands along his denim-clad thighs, and took a deep breath. "You're right," Blake said sadly. "I am in love with a ghost, but my heart belongs to the man he used to be. I knew I shouldn't have come here." Blake ran his hands through his hair before resting his forearms on his thighs and hanging his head. "You scare me, Ty."

Cautiously, Ty sat next to Blake and ran a soothing hand down Blake's back. "Why?"

"You make me feel things. Things I shouldn't be feeling." With his elbows on his knees, Blake hid his face in his hands, and Ty barely heard him mutter, "Things that could hurt you."

"I don't understand. I spent a week with you, and not once did I see anything in you but patience and compassion, even when I'd freak out and scream and rage at you. I don't believe you would ever hurt me."

"You're wrong!" Blake turned his head and glared at him. "Don't you get it? I brought Eli into my lifestyle. Before he met me, he was young, innocent, and I brought him into a world that killed him. A world I swore I would never enter again, and then you." Blake waved a hand toward Ty before resting his forearms back on his thighs and hanging his head. "I thought I could help you. Just one more time, I'd step into that role."

Ty's mouth fell open, his eyes wide. "Christ, you did help me," Ty said adamantly. "You gave me a chance to get my shit together, take a good look at myself, and because of you, I was able to let go some of my anger long enough to deal with it."

Blake let out a long, deep sigh and continued to stare at the floor.

When Blake didn't speak, Ty moved closer and wrapped an arm around Blake's waist and rested his head on Blake's shoulder. "Tell me what happened to Eli."

Blake clenched and unclenched his fists, then took a deep breath before speaking. "Eli and I had been together for about four years when we started going to this club called The Whip. Eli wasn't just my lover, my best friend, he was also my full-time sub. I'd been the one to introduce him to the lifestyle, but he was a natural." Blake chuckled quietly as if he were remembering a pleasant memory, then grew quiet briefly before continuing.

"There was this Dom, John Wood, and his sub, Dominick. We met shortly after we started going to the club. We all became friends. Eli really liked Dominick, and we all started hanging out together outside of the club. After a while, I noticed John staring at Eli a lot, but didn't think anything of it. My ego was pretty big, and I took it as a compliment. Eli was gorgeous, and when he submitted, he was stunning. I had this cocky attitude, preening with the attention John was showing toward Eli, because in my head, I had the best-looking boy as well as the best trained."

"Sounds like you were very proud of him."

Blake nodded. "I was. The first thing that started some warning sounds to buzzing in my head was when John began to dress Dominick like Eli, and then Dominick started to mimic Eli's movements and mannerisms. I was so arrogant I ignored the warning signs." Blake pressed the heels of his hands to his eyes.

"I can see why you would take that as a compliment." Ty rubbed a comforting hand in circles over Blake's back.

"Yeah, I did, and that was my first mistake." Blake sounded weary. He stood up, running his hands through his hair, and began to pace in Ty's small living room. "I was Eli's Dom. It was my job to protect him and keep him safe, but my fucking ego got in the way, and I didn't pay attention to the blaring alarms. By the time I did, it was too late. Eli and I stopped going to the club, broke off our friendship with John and Dominick, but it was too late."

Blake leaned against the wall, let out a long, deep sigh, and stared at the floor. "Three weeks later, I came home from work…." Blake swallowed hard, his hands curling into fists. "John somehow managed to convince Eli to let him in, and…." A deep, agonizing sound escaped Blake, and he slammed his fists against the wall. "The sick son of a bitch tried to force Eli to submit to him." Blake looked up at Ty with red-rimmed and pleading eyes. "This fucking lifestyle kills, and even knowing that, knowing what can happen, I didn't care. Being with you made me miss it. I still fucking crave it. Want it." Blake lowered his eyes and heaved a trembling sigh. "Being with you made me want all the things I had with Eli," Blake whispered, sounding defeated.

Ty launched himself off the couch and wrapped his arms around the grieving man. "There is nothing wrong with wanting those things. The lifestyle didn't kill Eli. That sick fuck did."

"But—"

"But nothing," Ty cut him off. "There are sick people in the world, Blake. It's a fucked-up fact of life. They are in churches, schools, daycares, and yes, in BDSM clubs, and they come from all walks of life." Ty held the trembling man tighter. "Poor, rich, religious, atheist, educated, dropouts, men, women, teens, straight, gay—no one group has exclusive rights on psychos. I am so very sorry for what happened to Eli, for what you lost. But it was *not* your lifestyle that killed Eli, it was a sick, twisted fuck named John Wood."

"I know that." Blake groaned. "I know that in my head, but my heart?" Blake shook his head. "It was my idea to take Eli to that club, my fault he met John Wood, and it was my job to protect my boy, and I didn't."

The heat of Ty's own tears rolled down his cheeks as he held onto a quietly sobbing Blake, whispering in a hoarse voice, "It's not your fault, Blake. You couldn't have known what Wood would do, and there is nothing wrong with wanting those things back." Ty tightened his hold. "Even after what Brian did to me, I still wanted what we'd had in the beginning. I still want those things."

A light went on, and it suddenly made sense. Ty had done the same thing Blake had done. He'd blamed everyone he'd met since leaving Brian for what the psychotic bastard had done to him. He'd denied himself what he truly wanted by never trusting a Dom fully again after Brian and had unwittingly put every Dom he met after that in the same class as Brian.

They clung to each other, Blake having to let go of the blame he had placed on the lifestyle he still wanted to live and Ty having to learn to stop blaming everyone in the lifestyle he craved for Brian's sins.

After the tears stopped falling and the sobs turned into even breaths, Blake whispered, "What now?"

Ty pulled back slightly, wiped first the wet trail left behind on Blake's cheeks and then his own. Gently, Ty pressed their lips together. Both groaned as the kiss deepened into a thorough exploration of each other's mouths. Ty cupped Blake's face in both of his hands and looked into dark-brown eyes. "Now I make you the pancakes I promised and we take it one step at a time."

Blake placed a tender kiss to Ty's lips. There was an uncertainty in Blake's eyes, but he nodded and allowed Ty to pull him into the kitchen.

CHAPTER
TWENTY-TWO

"PLEASE tell me you didn't pick out your wedding apparel," Aiden hooted from where he was lying on Lorcan's bed. "You look like Mel Brooks in *Blazing Saddles*." Aiden rolled across the bed, holding his stomach as he laughed. "Is that vest an exact replica?"

"Mama, three sons is enough for anyone, so I'm sure you won't mind if I choke that one," Lorcan grumbled, pointing at a still hysterically laughing Aiden.

"Oh, hush," Caroline James scolded. "Don't pay your brother no never mind. Just look at the way he's dressed." His mama waved a delicate hand in Aiden's direction before adjusting Lorcan's bowtie.

"Hey," Aiden complained, wiping the tears from his cheeks. "There is nothing wrong with my clothes."

"If you're going for the homeless guy look," Lorcan shot back.

"Aiden," their mama warned, "go change those jeans to ones with fewer holes and see if you can help Lenn and Cameron set up the chairs."

Aiden opened his mouth to complain but wisely closed it after the look Mama shot in his direction. Properly chastised, Aiden went to, hopefully, find some different jeans, but knowing the man as well as he did, Lorcan doubted it. Being the sweetest of the four boys, Aiden would win Mama's forgiveness for the homeless look he'd be sporting at the wedding.

Lorcan studied his reflection in the mirror. Black silk pants, matching black silk jacket with black velvet lapel, white ruffled shirt, and black-and-white vest. Aiden wasn't the only one Lorcan was going to choke. "Christ, Mama, I do look like Mel Brooks. What the hell was Conner thinking?"

"Oh, stop, you do not look like that short, pudgy man," Mama soothed. She went up on tiptoe and kissed his cheek. "My son is tall and so much better looking."

Lorcan pulled her into an embrace. "Do you think I'm doing the right thing, marrying Quinn?" he asked, suddenly serious. "What if I'm rushing into this?" Lorcan asked, voicing the fears that had settled into his gut and grown each day since the preparations for the wedding had begun.

Conner had been in his glory, planning every detail from the food, cake, music, to their wedding clothes. They had just received word earlier in the week that John's scan showed a possible tumor near the lumbar region of his spine, and he would be going for more tests next week. But Conner had stayed focused on the wedding, and Lorcan had given him free rein. Hell, he would have worn a rainbow clown suit to get married in if that was what Conner had wanted, thankful that the wedding kept Conner from sitting for too long and worrying.

"Baby," his mama said softly, pulling Lorcan from his musings, "I've known since you first came back home that you were in love with Quinn. I watched you together at the hospital, and I've seen the way the two of you naturally gravitate toward the other as if neither of you can stand to be too far away from the other. Do I believe you love each other? Yes. But only you can answer the question of whether *you* think you're rushing into marriage." Mama squeezed Lorcan tighter. "I knew your daddy all of two weeks before I married him. I was sure then, and thirty-two years later, I'm still sure."

Lorcan placed a kiss to the top of his mama's head before releasing her. He straightened his Mel Brooks vest and bowtie. "I've been in love with Quinn almost since the first moment I laid eyes on him, and that hasn't changed in nearly two years. C'mon," he said without a hint of hesitation. "Let's go start on my thirty-two years."

"And counting," his mama said with a laugh.

The fall weather, as Conner had predicted, with temperatures in the low seventies, the trees in their full glory of spectacular colors, and not a cloud in the azure-blue sky, was perfect. Conner had outdone himself. The large white tents set up in the yard were decorated with streamers of burgundy, bright gold, vibrant reds, and earthy greens that mirrored the flowers and candle arrangements on each china-covered table. Chairs were set up in aisles on the grassy side yard, with fancy bows of the same colors as the streamers on each end.

Nothing in the yard, however, could hold a candle to his sexy soon-to-be husband leaning against the railing of the back porch. Lorcan's heart skipped a beat and his breath caught in his throat when he saw Quinn standing there, dressed in the same wedding clothes as Lorcan was, with a brilliant smile on his face.

The silk pants and jacket with the black-and-white printed vest and tie didn't look as if they had come from a comedy. On Quinn, the material hugged his broad shoulders and chest, and the silk of his pants showed off his well-defined thighs, highlighting the man's large and stunning body. Christ, Lorcan was a lucky bastard.

Lorcan couldn't move, his body beginning to shake, and he could only stand and gawk at Quinn as he sauntered down the steps of the porch and made his way toward Lorcan.

"Mmm, mm, mm," Quinn hummed as he came up to Lorcan and pulled him into a tight embrace. Jolts of electricity shot down Lorcan's spine as Quinn nuzzled his neck, placing light kisses below his ear. "You look so gorgeous, baby," Quinn murmured against Lorcan's ear.

Quinn sealed their mouths together in a sweet but thorough kiss before Lorcan could return the compliment. Lorcan was breathless when Quinn showered his face with light kisses before returning to Lorcan's mouth for a deep and possessive kiss.

Lorcan, so consumed by the taste of his lover and the explorations of their tongues, hadn't heard the music begin to play and reluctantly ended the kiss when Mama tugged on his jacket.

"Save it for the honeymoon," she lightly chastised.

Aiden, in his predicted holey jeans but with an added sports coat over his T-shirt, looped his arm with Mama's and winked. "Pay attention, li'l brother. As soon as I help Mama to her seat, it's showtime."

"You mean *walk* me to my seat." Mama swatted Aiden playfully with her free hand, then looked between Quinn and Lorcan and nodded her approval before walking away with Aiden.

"Any second thoughts?" Quinn asked, entwining their fingers.

"Not a one," Lorcan said confidently.

As they walked down the aisle hand in hand, Lorcan beamed at his family. They had come to support him and share in the most important day of his life. As he met each of their eyes, if there were any misgivings that their son or brother was committing to another man or regret that there would be no grandchildren or nieces and nephews, Lorcan couldn't find it. Each smiling face looked at him with nothing but love. Conner and John sat with Mrs. Church, Clint, and the rest of the ranch hands, Conner dabbing at his eyes, and John held his hand tightly. Lorcan smiled when he remembered Quinn telling him about Conner's request. *"John and I want to be able to watch our only boy get married before we're too old to enjoy the party."* Conner had gotten his wish.

Their marriage wouldn't be recognized by the state of Oklahoma, but it didn't matter. They didn't need a representative from the state or an official from the church to give credibility to their commitment to one another. Lorcan and Quinn stood before their friends and family and read their vows to each other and to those who mattered the most.

Lorcan's knees were weak and he was trembling inside as he recited his vows, but his voice held steady as he looked into Quinn's blue eyes.

"I left home looking for adventure and acceptance, and what I found was the love of my life. There were times of uncertainty, happiness, heartache, and laughter. But through it all, the one constant, the one thing that never faltered, was my love for you. Today I commit myself to you freely and completely." Lorcan swallowed down the lump in his throat and, with a shaking hand, pulled the gold band from his pocket.

"Damn, there goes my twenty bucks," Lenn whispered.

Lorcan shook his head and smiled when Aiden whispered back, "I told you he wouldn't forget it."

Lorcan held out the ring to Quinn. "This ring is just a symbol of my commitment to you. The real commitment is safely tucked away in my heart and soul, and I give them both to you freely. They will forever belong to you and only you."

Quinn's eyes were wet with unshed tears as Lorcan placed the ring on his right hand. Quinn admired the ring briefly, then took a shuddering breath and met Lorcan's gaze.

"When I was growing up, I heard the taunts and hateful things the kids and some adults said about John and Conner. Not wanting to be at the other end of those words, I hid behind a lie and a premise that it was no one's business who I loved. It took losing you before I could step out of my self-imposed prison. John and Conner taught me what love is, but it took a desperate cowboy looking for adventure to teach me how to love and that real love is worth any amount of scorn."

Quinn pulled a matching band from his pocket and held it out to Lorcan. "When you left, I remember thinking I'd given you my heart and soul on a silver platter and that I wasn't ever getting them back. And now I know I don't ever want them back. They are yours forever. Lorcan, I'm a better man today because of you, and I promise to love you openly and proudly. My commitment to you is to spend the rest of my life cherishing you and our love."

Quinn fumbled to put the ring on Lorcan's finger, whether it was because Quinn's hands were trembling or Lorcan's had never stopped, he didn't know. Somehow he slid the ring onto Lorcan's finger, brought Lorcan's hand to his lips, and kissed the ring.

"I love you," Quinn said fiercely as he laid Lorcan's hand over his heart and pulled him into a tight embrace.

"I love you too," Lorcan replied just before Quinn took his mouth in a passionate kiss.

Cheers and applause went up around them, but Lorcan barely noticed as his husband deepened the kiss.

STRONG hands massaged Ty's shoulders seconds before Blake's whispered words tickled against his ear. "They look happy."

Ty reached up, cupping a hand around Blake's neck, holding him close as he watched a laughing Lorcan and Quinn feed each other cake. "Yeah, they do. It looks good on them."

"It looks good on you too," Blake murmured against Ty's neck.

He was happy. He and Blake had spent the last ten days talking, sometimes crying, and making each other feel good as often as they could. Ty had no idea where things were going to go between them. Blake had asked him to come to New York with him, and Ty had agreed to go for a couple of weeks. Ty wanted to be there to hold Blake's hand when he returned to the apartment full of memories.

Ty turned in Blake's arms and smiled. "It looks good on you too," Ty said before kissing Blake's smiling mouth.

"One step at a time, babe."

Ty's heart melted just a little more with the endearment. Hopefully one day, he'd hear Blake call him *boy*.

A WHISPERING PINES RANCH NOVEL

LORCAN'S DESIRE

SJD PETERSON

http://www.dreamspinnerpress.com

A WHISPERING PINES RANCH NOVEL
BOOK II

QUINN'S NEED

SJD PETERSON

http://www.dreamspinnerpress.com

SJD PETERSON, better known as Jo, hails from Michigan. Not the best place to live for someone who hates the cold and snow. When not reading or writing, Jo can be found close to the heater checking out NHL stats and watching the Red Wings kick a little butt. Can't cook, misses the clothes hamper nine out of ten tries, but is handy with power tools.

Visit Jo at http://www.facebook.com/SJD.Peterson; http://sjdpeterson. blogspot.com/; and http://www.goodreads.com/author/show/ 4563849.S_J_D_Peterson. Contact Jo at s_JO_d@comcast.net.

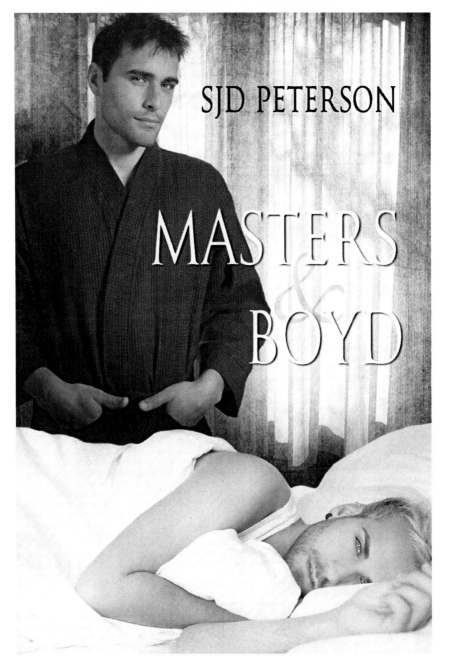